Rum Runner

Shirley F.B Carter

Goose River Press
Waldoboro, Maine

Library of Congress Card Number: 2025949337

ISBN: 978-1-59713-282-4

First Printing, 2026

Cover design by Kira Beaudoin.

Published by
Goose River Press
3400 Friendship Road
Waldoboro ME 04572
e-mail: gooseriverpress@gmail.com
www.gooseriverpress.com

Dedication

This book is dedicated to my daughters:

LAURA and MIA

who have consistently supported and assisted
my writing efforts.

And my sister

AUDREY E. BROWN (1930–2024)

who was my reliable critic and first reader
of all my published works.

Table of Contents

Other Books by Shirley F. B. Carter

Colored, of Course

The Roan

The Earl of Lee Heights

Acknowledgements

My debt of gratitude begins with generations of living and dead relatives and includes Worcester Public Schools teachers: specifically, the third grade Roosevelt Grammar school and the Grafton Street Junior High School English teachers.

For the completion of Rum Runner, I am very grateful for the professional support and guidance of Laurie Porter and Gabrielle Johansen.

Chapter One

Sunday dinner in the church hall was a collaborative feast of homemade comfort food. The meal had been served, and the women began their usual animated banter. No one was in a hurry to go home.

"It's those new people," Claire Holmes exclaimed. "They haven't showed up here yet, but they sure have money."

"Most of us who live in the Hollow never see them at our community church," Bridget O'Toole chimed in. "Some are very generous. I am making more money, too, filling specialty orders at the bakery."

"I saw a few new faces in the hardware store last week," interrupted Claire.

"Told them, 'You are not from the Hollow.' Without a bit of hesitation, they said, 'Why, yes, Mam, we came here to make money off the 'ole president's folly.' I knew just what they meant! My daughter is being courted by one of them newcomers. He's one o' them."

"He treating her good? Our own boys are in it, too. At least we have some idea what to expect from them 'cause we've known their families over time. These Johnny-come-latelys are here from Boston, New York and Lord knows where else." Caroline had to chuckle, even as she wagged her finger in warning.

As they cheerfully cleared and cleaned up, each of the women waved a hand or jumped into the lively discussion.

All but Marie Araujo. Her silence went unnoticed. She followed the conversation with wonderment. Has this whole town gone rum crazy? she wondered. Is my best friend in the business, too?

Marie left the church hall feeling pleased. She slid onto her bicycle, gracefully arranging her Sunday dress, and headed for the Hollow.

***

The Hollow was that part of Hyannis where generations of early settlers, indigenous people, runaway slaves and free men created close knit communities. Intermarriage was common. Hispaniola—and Portuguese-colonized island elders were generous and available to all the children. Marie's grandmother was a favorite—they called her Granny Araujo. She could be trusted and never divulged the private whispers of the children. Marie, when she was young, had told her about her special friend, George. "Granny, I love him. I know I can never win his heart. He loves the sea." Granny could hear the sadness in her voice and admired the wisdom of such a young soul.

From the early livelihoods of fishing and farming, some of the members of this community became business owners and lived off cottage industry, making all manner of things for sale. They ran laundries, did hauling, horticulture for hire, landscaping, maintenance, and municipal work. It was the very early White residents who dubbed this section of town "Happy Hollow."

Like their southern counterparts, they viewed people of color as "carefree, undisciplined and 'Happy' to live in high-priced and below standard houses." Satisfied to live humble, hard-working lives.[1]

Marie lived in that community, clinging to the old ways, the old culture, and the old people. She had left her childhood home as soon as she managed to make her own living by fishing. Her parents, eager to be American, had raised their child in a very restricted manner. After appreciating and gaining all she could from their care and consideration, she left them but remained in the Hollow. It allowed her to keep close to them and to her grandmother, who conveniently lived near her friend George's family, who were farmers and did hauling.

Her Granny had dancing eyes that revealed the mischievous girl who remained within the myriad wrinkles in her tan face. In good weather, Granny sat in her rocker on her porch. The oversized, custom-made chair accommodated her robust body and generous lap, broad enough to cuddle more than one child and still leave space even for a pre-teen.

Marie's best friend, George Winter, was one of Granny's favorites. Always independent, he became a successful fisherman. Tall, lean, bronze in winter, mahogany in summer, George had long brown curly hair. His clean-shaven face emphasized his chiseled cheekbones. When the season was at its peak, he could afford to hire extra hands. Marie worked for him even when he didn't ask for help. She would just be there. Without verbal acceptance or refusal, they worked

---

[1] Harold Tobey, *The Barnstable Patriot*, May 29, 2020.

together, creating free time to share. Her unspoken salary was half the day's profit. Time spent together was special: no agenda, lots of walking the dunes, enjoying the roses, eating beach plums, and picnicking by the sea.

In the early 1920s, change was emerging on the Cape. The White population was establishing new industry, building new homes and schools, flourishing. Buying and selling land spawned new, lucrative ventures. Marie teamed up with a local woman who started her own real estate business. Hanging out with Jenny Strong and keeping up with the politics and commercial changes affecting the Cape fascinated Marie. She shared her thoughts and dreams with George. He admired and complimented her on her ambition and serious, almost secret aspirations.

"George, the railroad is expanding," she told him. "From that first burst of newcomers and business at the glass factory in Sandwich, the Cape is no longer just a seasonal destination for the rich. It's a place of growing commerce and opportunity for White people with visions of profit. Jenny and I can see the good and the sad in it. Tourism is a lucrative business, but we year-round locals won't be the ones getting rich. There are always winners and losers when big money gets involved. Jenny is teaching me. She invites me to go along when she meets and befriends people. She calls them 'tycoons.' "

George listened, admiring, but his interest wasn't in politics or big money. He loved fishing and shared what he earned with his grandparents and with Granny Araujo, too. His thoughts about money were seasonal. Stormy weather, winter or summer, made the season good or bad. He was a year-round fisherman.

Marie had turned heads from the time she was a tiny girl. Her parents' investment in assimilation taught her to stand tall, walk proudly and adorn herself in ways that flattered her natural tan skin. She was enrolled in the best local schools, blessed with piano and dance lessons and taught to listen carefully, speak only when spoken to, and gauge everyone as untrustworthy until proven otherwise. Good nutrition, good habits, and knowledge were requirements. Marie learned and listened and, ultimately, bristled against the household rules. Her parents labored constantly toward perfection. "You will always have to work longer and harder to compete because you are not White," they told her.

Marie's happiest times were with her grandparents. Her other happy times were spent with George, Jenny, and the ladies at church.

The church women swapped recipes, complained and bragged about husbands and children, and admired the single women and business women for their fortitude. In the mid-1920s, it wasn't common for women to own or manage shops. Polly Allen was a first generation American, but her English accent could fool you. She was a long-time resident and the proud owner of Queen's Sandwich Shop. Her investment capital, and her accent, had been passed on by her parents, who had fled Great Britain decades before. Political unrest, the big stink of 1858, when sewage fumes in central London had inspired many Britons to leave, along with the potato famine in Ireland had brought Polly's and Bridget's relatives to Cape Cod.

Bridget O'Toole managed the Bakers Dozen Bakery

on Main Street, number 13. She alone was responsible and managed the business well. The absentee owners, the Batchelder family, entrusted her with all decisions, including their banking and investing. The family had owned the bakery for generations. Bridget had spent her youth and all her adult life working there. Her skills not only included specialty baking but also scrupulous money management. Her red hair and fiery disposition could intimidate a banker, politician or any other fool who thought she was a pushover. She often boasted, "Go ahead, underestimate me. That will be entertaining!"

Devon White had come into home ownership and developed it into a shop. Cottage industry was respectable, and on the Cape, it became profitable in summer. She made quilts, showcased jewelry made by other craftswomen, and added delicious homemade fudge that brought her regular customers to White's Sweet Shop.

Caroline Wolf's laundry business was passed on to her by her mother, a Wampanoag woman who had married a man known to be a runaway slave from down south. The well-established business drew many rich families, who paid fair prices and benefited from the excellent work Caroline and her mother maintained over the years.

There were proud fishermen's wives like Mary Helen Pinkney and Annie Sullivan, who could bargain and barter better than their husbands. Homemakers like Hazel Jones offered quiet logic when conversations became unruly or testy.

Claire Holmes was a clerk in the hardware store. Her brother, Ernest Bearse, went into the military, leaving the shop short-handed, and as a courtesy, she re-placed him. Claire did such an admirable job that the boss respected her and kept her on. The owner paid her wages equal to those of the men. She got along well in the male environment.

This winter of 1923, much of the conversation was about the "President's Noble Experiment": Prohibition.

Chapter Two

"Hi, everybody. It's so good to be back home!" Marie burst into the cool church hall.

"Welcome back, you vagabond. What the dickens do you do in New York for days? That adventurous spirit of yours scares me sometimes." Polly Allen meant well, but she was curious about Marie: so young, going off alone for days at a time.

Annie Sullivan chimed in. "I think you're envious, Polly. We all love hearing what news or nonsense Marie brings to us—when she tires of the big city and comes back home where she belongs." Laughter brought everyone's attention back to Marie, who explained.

"Oh, Polly, I don't go by myself. I'm an apprentice to my good friend, Jenny Strong. We stay right in the city, in nice hotels paid for by her clients. It's legal stuff: deeds, buying and selling. I carry paperwork, and Jenny sometimes goes to the courthouse while I read newspapers and make sure we schedule our meetings and train tickets in a timely manner. I'm her clerk. It pays well, and in winter when I'm not out on the boats, it gets me out in the world. Prohibition has made the city lively. Everyone has money to spare, and everyone knows where to buy bootleg liquor. We had dinner with an Englishman, and I asked him about prohibition there. He looked at me like I had hit him with a paddle and grunted, 'We'll never have such a thing in Great Britain! We gentlemen know how to imbibe sensibly.' I felt like maybe I should apologize, but Jenny brushed it off like she had expected as much from him."

Polly was smiling now. "Oh, we had our comeuppance about alcohol years back," she said, her lingering British accent more intense than usual. "The new mills, the poor working class and beer! The women were trying to put a stop to the drunkenness, suffering as they did when their husbands sank into habitual violence when they were drunk. It all resolved when the upper classes got involved. No, we never outlawed drinking, and we never will."

"It's evident in New York that prohibition may be here to stay," said Marie. "There are clubs everywhere, dance halls with rowdy fun music. And the fashion! I've never seen so much glitter."

"So, it's not all work. Sounds like you been in those clubs!" Bridget O'Toole was half teasing but clearly wanted to know.

Marie answered her seriously. "One of Jenny's clients wanted to venture in and see what was going on. He invited us to join him, then escorted us out rather quickly. I wanted to dance all night. The music was wonderful! But Jenny and I work well together. She's a serious businesswoman. This last trip was a real adventure for both of us."

Chapter Three

"Marie, there will be one more meeting this evening," Jenny said as they sat in the hotel lobby. "Mr. Beaumont, from Chicago, was referred to me by our last customer. I promised him I would squeeze him in before we leave tomorrow. Both men are investing in the same property. That's probably him now." She stood up as a tall man with fair hair approached them.

"Good evening, Miss Strong," he said. "It is so good of you to see me on such short notice. I am John Beaumont, Mr. Grant's partner. We've made the decision to work together on this project."

"This will not take long," Jenny replied. "I adjusted much of the paperwork while Mr. Grant was here. My assistant here, Miss Araujo, and I will be leaving for Hyannis early tomorrow. I can file the completed document there and you will be all set."

Marie promptly produced the file from her satchel. Mr. Beaumont carefully read through the documents and then removed a pen from his suit pocket to sign them.

"It's been a pleasure doing business with you, sir," said Jenny.

"I am so fortunate to have caught you before you left. This has been so efficient that I now have the evening free. I've often wanted to visit one of the clubs where alcohol is still abundant. Would you consider it too bold of me to invite you for a brief visit, to satisfy my curiosity? I understand they have live bands and doormen to keep patrons safe from harm. I believe unescorted women frequently attend in small groups. I'd be honored to escort you tonight."

The two women looked at one another. "That would be quite an opportunity for us," Jenny said. "What do you say, Marie?"

"I've heard some of the music," she answered. "It's wonderful to dance to. It's been a long time since I visited a dance hall. Let's do it."

"There's a club near this hotel," said John Beaumont. "My colleagues told me to use a password at the door to foil any Probis. Those narcotics agents are making a name for themselves in Chicago, raiding halls."

"Are agents active in New York as well?" Jenny felt a bit of caution rise. "Here it all seems so common and carefree."

"I think it's more part of the charm or identity of each club to have a password, rather than a fear of being raided."

He led them out of the hotel and out onto Broadway, where they walked for only a few minutes before he pointed to a darkened doorway. "Hold onto the rail, ladies. There may be more steps before we are let inside."

"May I call you Mr. B.? I'm Marie," she said. "Formalities seem out of place right now."

His smile confirmed his approval. "Of course. It fits the occasion."

He rapped loudly on the door, which opened to allow only a slit of light until Mr. B. whispered "Starlight." They were then quickly ushered inside. Jenny reached for Marie's hand as they followed closely behind their escort.

"More steps, ladies," he called back. "Be careful."

Marie was still holding Jenny's hand as they descended the last step. "Oh, my," she said. "It's so dark, but I can clearly see the dancing polka dot lights. They're like crazy fireflies swimming across the walls and ceiling and everywhere!"

They began to weave their way around tables. Until their eyes adjusted, they were cautious in the dim light, thickened by cigarette smoke and dappled with flashes from a spinning crystal ball. Mr. B. found a table near the small stage, where a man playing a clarinet struck a loud wailing sound like a mournful human voice. When the rest of the band joined in, the music took on a life of its own.

"The Lindy!" Marie couldn't bring herself to take a seat.

"Would you ladies join me in a drink? Perhaps a gin and tonic."

"Marie, please sit down," Jenny pleaded.

But gliding across the dance floor came a young man with Harlem in his handsome face and Harare rhythm in his hips. He reached out a hand and pulled Marie onto the dance floor. The razzmatazz that followed made other dancers give the floor to the shimmying, knee smacking, hip gyrating couple whose shoulder shaking and happy faces improvised the Lindy with abandon. Band members grinned their approval and, when the music paused, the audience as well as the other dancers applauded.

Flushed and beaming, bits of light dotting her face, Marie joined her party at the table while her dance partner disappeared into the crowd. Few words were spoken while the trio ogled the crowd and sipped their drinks. The band's short recess revived Marie and she jumped to her feet. Mr. B. joined her, assuring her that he was not great at improvising but would do his best with the Lindy.

When they returned, he offered his hand to Jenny. "Come join me. The music is wonderful!"

"Mr. Beaumont, I'm sorry. I have no idea how to do this. My feet have been tapping—that's all I can manage."

When the dance floor cleared at the band's next intermission, Jenny guided Marie to the exit, Mr. B. behind them. The three mounted the stairs and, with a generous smile, the burly doorman quickly cracked the door open so they could scurry into the quiet of the night.

"I could have danced all night!" Marie was so animated that Jenny frowned at her, convinced the liquor had influenced her friend.

But Marie only laughed. "I'm not intoxicated, Jenny. It's the music! It was so wonderful. Thank you, Mr. B. You are a good sport, a good dancer, *and* a good customer."

"This has been a wonderful evening, ladies. I am not sure I wanted it to end, but I am thankful to have spent the time with you."

They quickly reached the hotel.

"This was an unexpected pleasure," Jenny said. "Sorry to have cut it short; we have an early departure scheduled tomorrow. It was splendid of you to escort us this evening."

***

That next Sunday, the ladies at church did not hear all the details, but they were still laughing after the work was done as Marie entertained them, mimicking the dance tunes, the shimmying, and some fancy leg moves. There was a plan to bring a gramophone to the next meeting to add more fun to the cleanup chores. It did not happen, but the thought of it sent everyone home smiling.

Frequently, when Marie was not at the dinners, she was the topic of conversation.

"Marie noticing the speakeasies in New York is but little when we open our eyes to what's happening here," Polly said one week. "Business is flourishing, farms are being sold for tons of money, and alcohol is fueling all of it! Even the sheriff is involved!" Polly kept up with the politics and changes happening in Hyannis and out at the Port. "Now I'm thinking Marie is in it somehow. Ever notice how she gets off the train in Wareham? Jenny Strong comes straight to Hyannis, where her office is. Not Marie. Wonder what kind of 'business' she does there. I am sure her pal, George, meets her there."

Devon White cleared her throat loudly to interrupt the gossiping.

"Ladies, I know why Marie gets off in Wareham. Tourists shop there at the gateway to the Cape. They are attracted by the Indians and other crafts people selling their wares, authentic and junk. She buys good handmade baskets, shawls, and jewelry for me. I pay

14

her a commission, and she does meet up with George Winter. They arrange it ahead of time."

Polly, a bit resentful of the interruption, added one more observation about Marie. "They are a curious couple, George and Marie. She obviously loves and adores him. But his only love interest is the sea."

Devon jumped in. "Now *that's* a dangerous love affair. The sea is an equalizer. No matter who you are, lowly fisherman or rich yachtsman, you'd better respect her! She can be calm, violent, magnificent, luminous, raging."

No one compared Marie to the sea.

"There'll be no babies from that relationship!" concluded Mary Helen Pinkney. And, with a nod or a snicker, all agreed.

But Devon didn't let it end there. "What's wrong with loving someone and not being all about romance and babies? I think George and Marie have mutual respect. Their kind of love is called platonic."

The other women looked at her as if she were speaking some unknown form of English. They left in silent agreement. Marie was certainly an unusual young woman.

Chapter Four

Marie could sell the beauty of the Cape with her words. Jenny harnessed this skill whenever they were together selling real estate. Jenny would give Marie the keys to a house for sale, have her meet with the prospective buyer, and feel confident that the house would be sold before the day ended.

"If you have never spent time on Cape Cod, you have missed the dunes, beach grass, endless waves, and sandy beaches," Marie would tell a buyer, closing her eyes savoring the things she loved. "The freshwater ponds are plentiful, too. Walking on the dunes, you will see wild roses and edible plums. The alkaline soil is what makes these beautiful hydrangeas soooo blue. Notice the consistent gray shingles on the houses? The salty air colors them and you never have to paint them. They are weatherproof."

Enchanted, the buyer would purchase postcards to prove to friends how correctly Marie had described their soon-to-be new home.

Conversation at church had caught up with the times: dance halls, the music, the fashion, the wild abandon. And there were times when Marie found herself telling Hyannis news and updates to some of the homemaker mothers. They did not avidly read the newspapers and truly were at home most of the time.

Hazel Jones was serious when she reacted to Marie's enthusiasm. "Nothing much has or will happen here in the Hollow. We're the same tried and true folk, born and bred here. Our forefathers were traders, fishermen, farmers, and immigrants from places having troubles all over. I am proud to be part Wampanoag. We're the original people, and we're still here."

She spoke the truth, and no one contradicted her. "Folks in this part of Hyannis are long-standing home-owners. The same families have lived, worked, and died here. The Oak Neck Cemetery is like a park, where people have picnics. If only downtown, the farms and the Port were that stable."

Polly Allen felt the need to update any of the mothers who were still oblivious to the big picture. "Marie, I am sure you know by now that the politicians and the Coast Guard are figuring out how to get in on the money. They go blind when the green is shared."

Annie confessed, "My husband, Howard, has managed to sock away a sweet pile and feels as proud as punch about having folding money in his pocket. Marie, you know he's been working on the fishing rig with George for years. As generous and fair as young George is, we have never had so much money on hand as we do now. Our local men are competing for the same things those fancy newcomers are, just wanting to care for their families. Rum running is a leveler. Our fishermen can be equal breadwinners and feel respected by these competitors. I have never seen Howie so happy. I think money makes him feel dignified!"

Marie did know. And Marie worried. "Our men are out there fishing, meeting the regular customer demands while competing with fast boats—men with guns—who are running fine wines and rum here from as far away as Newfoundland," she said. "Those men aren't fishing—they're using their money to pay off the police and the Coast Guard."

"I had no idea our men were at such risk." Mary Helen Pinkney was aghast and wanted to hear more about what had Polly and Marie so worked up. "What happens if they get caught? I haven't heard one thing about all of this."

Bridget O'Toole spoke up. "I haven't spoken to anyone about this, but I got the fright of my life a few days ago, Mary Helen. I saw strange men hanging 'round the storage shed behind the bakery. When I see one of 'em had a key, I watched. They were busy inside, and I ran off to find my grandpa's shotgun. No bullets in it, but before I confronted them, I went to the shed with it slung by my side. The man who had the key called my name! Begged me to hear him out. Told me he was young Jeffrey, grandson of old Mr. Batchelder. Said he and his fellows were using the old shed to store rock salt. Invited me in to prove his claim and offered me a cut in the sale. He was shaking so much, I just stared him down and left."

All the women held silent for long while. Bridget released a big sigh. She could exhale now that she had shared the incident. Glancing at the others, feeling their empathy, she continued.

"The following day when I saw them, I recognized one of our own boys, Nick Bassett: old family. I called him out and demanded he tell me what in damnation they were doing with all that rock salt. He was so excited to explain. He's one of them, a rum runner. Says boys have been getting arrested, and they have to evade the Coast Guard. Stuff they're selling is mighty expensive liquors and imported wines. If it's confiscated, it's resold by the guardsmen. So, our boys bundle the liquor, weight it down with rock salt, attach a familiar buoy, and when they spot the authorities, they toss it overboard. Then they wave and smile, act like the fishermen they really are. After, they go back, spot their buoy. The salts dissolved and they pull up their stash!"

The women were fascinated. Marie soberly recounted a worrisome thing she had recently heard. "George knows about the imported expensive liquor from Europe, and how the boys dump weighted heavy bundles overboard even at a loss rather than get arrested. But now, since the money and the stakes have risen, pirates are raiding fishing boats, searching for hidden alcohol, and they are armed devils."

The church hall became hushed as each woman took in the gravity of the situation. It was after a lengthy pause that Polly, the owner of the sandwich shop, spoke up to try to lighten the mood. "Those rich guys with the fast boats, gun owners with plenty of green, come into my shop. They're easy to spot: picking up large orders their wives have requested, acting loud and bold like they own the shop. I have 'em wait their turn, take my time, let 'em know I got other customers besides them. When they leave, grumbling because they had to wait, I smile, and they tell me to keep the change."

That shifted the mood, and there was more conversation about the wives of the men who were flaunting their money and demanding special service and attention. Claire Holmes had met them in the hardware store. "These rich women are eager to ask me for help and are genuinely amazed and appreciative of how much information and skill a female clerk can share."

Devon, the craftswoman, admitted that she had befriended some of the new monied ladies. "I find them quite interesting," she said. "And they're good return customers. Some come in with their servants. Load them down with the purchases. I like the maids. Many are colored and they come in on their own after seeing the variety of things I sell. Business is booming."

Everyone who spoke up was given serious attention by the others, and the stay-at-home mothers fully respected for their modest awareness and honest opinions.

"Now do not get Bridget stirred up about our vanishing farms," teased Polly. "That red hair is a warning. A tongue lashing from her will not quickly be forgotten." In the women's group, conversation rarely centered on ethnicity, but there were comments that showed ethnicity was recognized. "She took on one of the founding fathers when he was bragging to a reporter about how tourists and rich landowners are buying up farmland and improving the Cape."

Bridget spoke right up. "It is true. I told them, 'Farmers are the salt of the earth.' I interrupted the whole meeting! They could not stop me from telling it as it is. Old Joe Hull set the bar high for farmers. Good people, important people. If he was still alive, he would not be a sellout. When money replaces God, we are doomed to hell and damnation! Those rich bastards shun us and allow their children to run rampant even in the Catholic church. Why, St. Francis Xavier now has tours for 'visitors.' " She was still on a tear when she was interrupted by the sight of leftover strawberry shortcake that Mary Helen slid smackdab in front of her.

The old farmers and town folk had become leery of land-grabbing strangers. Marshland as well as farmland was being converted to large family compounds with mansions that included beachfront. Fast-talking sharks bought poor farmers' lots for a pittance, then sold the land for thousands.

Marie bragged to the group, "I can spot a phony or a crook *before* they begin behaving badly. If somebody in the Hollow tries to initiate a crooked deal, I confront them, expose them, and warn others about their shady deals. The Hollow is *my* community."

No sharks had attempted to buy any of Marie's family's land. "My family immigrated from Hispaniola, or whatever was left of it after colonization," she said. "For all I know, I may be Taino. So many of us here have mixed blood. Granny still speaks Portuguese, uses Spanish for some words, especially food, and sings French lullabies. She feels bad about my parents only using English and wanting to be proud Americans. Culture matters, and you can see it and feel it in the Hollow. My George's grandparents escaped slavery here in the States. His grandpa speaks Spanish and French as well as English. The old ones have held onto the old and embraced the new. That's how I want to live my life."

Chapter Five

It was one of *her* majestic April days. The *sea* was calm, sun shining in a cloudless blue sky. George set out to catch fish. The dock was jammed with more strange boats than he had ever seen. Colorful fancy yachts bobbed together like bath toys. George greeted the few fishermen whose rigs he recognized. He had taken a liking to a few of the new folks. He was curious about them and they about him. They crossed paths on the wharves and in taverns. Their exchanges were usually rough, bawdy, and full of laughter. Humor was shared along with good food. When the men from the Hollow met each other on the docks after a night of drinking more than eating, storytelling, and sometimes brawling, they were affable, their lifelong friendships easy. But the new men were aloof the next day, giving George only polite nods of recognition while they tended to their sloops and yachts.

This morning, Annie Sullivan's husband, Howard, hollered over to George, "Wow, the pleasure boats and the fishermen all want to take advantage of this beautiful day, even before the summer folks arrive."

He and George sized up the day's situation. "I'm going to catch blues today," George decided. "One person alone can easily manage my boat. The big fishing rigs need extra hands."

"I'll hire on to a big rig," Howard said. "I'll see you later."

George waved and set off. He headed out, continuing beyond the line of noisy boat traffic to where he often caught the elusive, feisty bluefish. Today, he would dry and stow his nets, use his poles instead. George welcomed the challenge. He had a special customer, a chef who made the best bluefish pâté on the Cape. This customer always paid well for his blues, no matter the size of the batch.

In serene waters, he lingered well into late afternoon, though he didn't find a single blue. *Oh, well,* he thought, *the sun will be setting soon and I'm far from land. Can't even see the tip of Provincetown.*

He had allowed himself to drift past Truro while watching a magnificent pod of whales, attracted by a school of larger fish. Their sound was music, but just as he set sail for home, a thunderous racket ended the tranquility. A huge whaling ship had appeared, the powerful engines creating a wake that rocked George's fishing boat. He quickly gave way, yet the ship turned to head him off.

Damn, do they think my little boat is going to net the fish before they reach the whales?

Using both motor and sail, he dodged left then right, moving as swiftly as possible, but to no avail.

They intend to swamp me!

No sooner had he come to that conclusion that he realized how close he had come to the whales. The last thing he saw clearly was a man on deck, pointing a rifle at him as the larger boat rammed his craft mid-stern. He dove, watching the shadow of bullets whiz by as he dove deeper and deeper.

Down he went into darkness. As a kid, he had been one of those brown skin boys in raggedy, cutoff shorts who entertained tourists who threw coins into the deep harbor where the ships anchored. The visitors marveled at how the boys retrieved all the coins, shared them, and disappeared as quickly as they had appeared.

Now George swam, making his way underwater until he surfaced to take his first breath in the center of the pod of whales. Neither he nor the whales were safe until darkness fell. The men on the marauding whaler harpooned their catch, never looking for the foolish fisherman they considered a nuisance.

Back at the harbor in Hyannis, Howie searched for George's boat. He concluded that he must have found a less crowded dock. When he saw Marie, he was sure she would know where he had come in.

"Why, no, Howie, it's already dark," she said. "No matter what other dock he might lay in, he should be in town by now. He and I planned to have dinner together. He never forgets."

Their eyes locked. In unison, in hushed voices, they whispered, "Coast Guard."

In the water, George was cold, fighting with all his might to swim towards the twinkling shore. The rocking of his body, the sound of the surviving whales, matched his acceptance of his fate. "I'll keep moving until ..."

"Hey, man, keep swimming!" Voices called out to him. He had been spotted by a pleasure boat full of teenagers, drawn close to the pod of whales. It was dark, and they were lost. For hours, their anxious, affluent parents had been worrying at the Coast Guard to search for them. Instead, the Guard had followed regular protocol, not considering the youths' absence an emergency until nightfall. Now, as a Coast Guard vessel bore down upon them, the young people made frantic gestures, pointing at George and shouting to the rescue party: "There's a man out there! Hurry, he's alive!"

George, exhausted but still moving, was blinded by the beam of light from the ship. Guardsmen reached to pull him aboard, carefully placing him on the deck and stripping him of his wet clothing, right down to his water-logged shoes. As quickly as a piece of clothing was removed, it was replaced with warm, dry cloth until he was swaddled head to toe like an infant. As the rescue boat led the teenagers' yacht to shore, George was administered skilled first aid to ward off hypothermia. He allowed himself to close his eyes, remembering a time when Granny Araujo had held him on her lap, rocking him gently, allowing his tears to fall unwitnessed.

Word spread quickly once they docked. The worried folks on the Hyannis pier cried with joy. Marie and Howard leaped into action.

"I'll rustle up some dry clothes for George and meet the ship," said Howie. "He'll be darned cold. Likely naked if he was in the water."

Marie agreed. "I'll head for his house and get a space heater going."

At the rescue boat, Howie bundled George into a warm coat, set him into his car and brought him home, where Marie was waiting. Seeing his house with lights on, George sat up abruptly. His eyes brimmed with reluctant tears.

With an excellent sense of timing and courtesy,

Howard left the two alone. George reached to give Marie a long, sustained hug. Her body quivered, gripped with a chill. She rewarded him with a bashful kiss, and then he was able to release her. Over warm mugs of hot chocolate, they huddled by the heater, and George told Marie the story of what had happened to him. Neither of them ever shared the details with the folks in the Hollow.

Word got out, and the story grew in every dimension.

"George Winter's boat got swamped by a school of whales!"

"No, a whaling ship harpooned George's boat. Tried to kill him!"

"George fell asleep looking for bluefish. Must have been drunk. How else could he have wrecked his damned boat? He's one of the best sailors I know!"

Tall tales circled Hyannis for several years.

That space heater hadn't been filled with whale oil. Fossil fuels were gaining popularity, and peak whaling days were ebbing. Yet every part of the whale was still marketable. Competition among whalers had not seemed like a big issue to George, but the school of fish that lured the whales also lured big whaling vessels. He was neither a threat to commercial fishing boats nor whalers. Desperation and guns now accompanied Prohibition. As he shopped for a new, faster boat, he investigated the rum business. With his meager savings and a small loan, he bought a good, seaworthy boat.

***

Summer came on quickly, and tourists continued to

boost the economy. George met a fellow named Bill Millett, from Eastham. He came to Cape Cod to be a turnip farmer. George's relatives had developed a now famous yellow turnip, popular on the East Coast. The two men commiserated about low farming profits and the development of farmland into housing by New York corporations.

"At first they were building fancy summer homes," said George. "Now it's year-round beachfront luxury compounds."

Bill knew farming was not his best option. "I've heard about a crew organizing here in Hyannis," he told George. "Importers of fine wines and liquors from France arrive here, and the goods are being shipped to be sold in New York. Ships with international credentials can't be touched by the U.S. Coast Guard, and their captains are aware of this loophole. They rendezvous with local rum runners, exchange large sums of money, and have safe passage even in Cape Cod waters. I know the days of bathtub gin are long over, but this crew only buys the best stuff from people who have lots of cash and can afford to pay top price."

George wanted to know more about this crew. The next time he and Bill met again, it was on the docks. Unable to secure a job on a farm, Bill had been meeting up with fishermen. He'd gone out on a few ships and tried his hand at hauling nets and getting his sea legs.

"So glad to see you, George!" Bill said. "I've been invited to a meeting. Fella's name is Patrick Killcarney. Calls himself Ricky. This is big. They're organizing, have lawyers, and need connections to unload the stuff locally. I know I'm never going to make a living fishing. It literally makes me sick!" Bill laughed. "Everybody and his brother are in the business, making decent money. That includes sheriffs, the Coast Guard, and politicians. You have that nice fast new boat. What do you think about teaming up? I'm sure Mr. Ricky will be happy to meet you. We're meeting next Monday at the Old Falmouth Inn."

George listened carefully and let Bill know he would give the proposal serious consideration. He wanted to talk with Marie.

They met at Granny Araujo's. "I'm tempted and excited," he told the two women. "Plenty of fishermen like me are also rum running. It's part of every conversation. We'd still fish for a living. Winters, we limit how far we go out. These transactions Bill is talking about are near shore. Some of the new guys have rigged their boats with fast engines, patching together aircraft engines from the war. I introduced myself to some of them, know some of them by name. They're a shifty kind of sailor. Lone wolfs doing those long runs to Newfoundland."

Granny noticed the gleam in his eye. "It's that *man* thing that men fall for," she told Marie later. "He is liking the challenge too much."

Marie knew George already had good connections with the suppliers and knew who was making the best quality local gin. Before the designated meeting, George confided to Marie, "I'm going to go. No one has approached me before this turnip farmer. He seems like a decent sort. Trustworthy."

Marie told him her gut feelings. "You men get bamboozled into risky stuff and fast money. It's a lure, a bit like the sea. You know darned well the sea not only offers a good living, but also tranquility, beauty and challenge. But she can beguile you, too, tempt you to go beyond your known limits. Those majestic sunrises can forecast killer storms by evening."

George listened, taking in every word. He knew she feared for him after his encounter with the whalers. And she never failed to compliment him. "George," she said, "You are an honorable man. Flirting with the law can ruin your good reputation."

That earned her a huge smile. "Marie, you are good at seeing people and situations that are shady. I'd like you to meet these fellows, Bill Millett and the guy setting up this meeting. His name is Patrick Killcarney. I met him briefly when he extended me an invitation. What do you say, partner? Dinner Monday night at the Old Falmouth Inn?"

Chapter Six

The Inn's large dining room reserved for the business meeting was filled with folks from the community: immigrants, the formerly enslaved, prospectors. There, too, were the nouveau riche, brandishing their prosperity. A smaller dining room held the tourists and overnight lodgers. George and Marie recognized the politicians, and the undertaker, and some of the year-round wealthy homeowners. Conversations were muted as people mingled with those with whom they were familiar. There was none of the bantering, the raucous laughter, or the loud choral singing so common in the local taverns.

Mr. Patrick Killcarney stood near a small platform, greeting guests. His trim, lanky body allowed one to imagine him a champion tennis player. His pinstriped seersucker jacket complemented his crisp white trousers and polished white leather shoes. He was tall, with a stern, ruddy face, well-tamed silver curly hair, and erect posture. He was unmistakably in charge.

As everyone settled at tables, a man Marie recognized as a real estate lawyer addressed Mr. Killcarney. "Ricky, what do you think about all the year-round houses being built in the Port?"

The question was purely rhetorical. It gave the

lawyer the privilege to bid the meeting begin.

"Ricky" flashed a broad smile, and in a loud voice, responded, "Carpet bagging is not on the agenda!" He held up his hands in a gesture for quiet, waiting until all talking ceased.

Marie tapped George's foot with her toe to draw his attention away from the basket of hot rolls being deposited on the starched white tablecloths, amidst glistening cut glass tumblers and an array of silverware.

"He's arrogant," she managed to whisper.

"We are here this evening to secure a talented crew of boatsmen to bring valuable, delicate products to shore for transport." The businessman's voice commanded the room as waitstaff poured ice water and placed family-style bowls of salad and golf ball-sized pats of butter on the tables. "Speed and skill are paramount. You have all been recommended by your close associates to be well-suited for this endeavor, and those chosen will be very well-paid! As you enjoy this fine meal I have provided, be thinking of questions I might answer that will bring us to a lucrative, cooperative business agreement. Welcome to The Crew."

The lavish meal was served with expensive red and white wines, matched to the filet mignon and the fish.

"That man means business," Marie told George as she cut into her steak. "Looks like he has already paid off the powers that be. His heart is cold."

"Are you saying he's not to be trusted?" George was familiar with the shrewd version of manhood society placed on men, especially when they were afforded opportunities to be successful breadwinners.

"No, George, I'm saying that he's obviously more

interested in money than in people.”

Marie knew George had made up his mind to join. He was among the first to ask specific questions.

“How far from shore will we meet up with these supply ships?” He had already assumed they would be the large international vessels Bill Millett had mentioned. George wondered if his boat would qualify.

“Right offshore from the British ships,” Killcarney answered. “You fellows running from Newfoundland need a better fleet. Only heaven knows how you’ve been successful up to this point.” Ricky had done his research. He named the speed boats that were making that run. “For you fellows, we hope to lower the risk by anchoring offshore. Any seaworthy craft can quickly get ashore. We have trucks and fast drivers waiting near the beach. They are efficient, knowledgeable and know many of your constables. They’re armed against the fools who want to be land pirates. We’ve considered every detail. And we pay well.”

George was no longer chatting with Marie. He made haste to beckon Bill to their table so they could confer, and so Marie could have some contact with Bill.

Those interested in signing up were invited to leave their contact information at a table near the exit. George and Bill joined the line.

***

On Marie and George’s next visit to the Hollow, they stopped by to see Granny Araujo. The cool evening breeze drove them from the porch into Granny’s kitchen. She was still in charge in that space, no matter her ninety-plus years. They followed her as she scuffed along, barely lifting her slippered feet from the worn wooden floor. She rocked like a skater in slow motion, minding that her full-length dress didn't cause a stumble.

"George, you're one o' them now! That dancing excitement in your eyes. The challenge and competition lures men to be adventuresome and rash!" She reached into one of her big apron pockets and handed Marie a small bundle of home-made cookies wrapped in a cloth napkin. "I tucked them away in case a young one stopped by while I was on the porch."

Granny bid them sit down while she put the kettle on for tea. This visit would be a bit longer than the planned "stopping by" George and Marie had intended.

"Say, Granny, did you notice who drove us here?" George asked, not wanting to be the sole topic of the conversation. "Who was at the wheel? We didn't ride bikes or get dropped off by Howie today."

"You drove here, Marie?" Granny had known George was teaching Marie to drive, but she was quite excited to hear the news. "I'm sure you won't have any trouble getting your license."

That did turn the conversation, and they began to talk about the many new ways in which women had begun to assert themselves, taking on roles once dominated by men.

"It took a heap of effort to get the vote," Granny said with pride. "There'll be no stopping us now!"

Long after the first cup of tea, George and Marie rose to leave. As she bid them goodbye, Granny wrapped herself in a blue and white crocheted shawl, taking a good look from the porch to watch Marie make an elegant turn and drive away. She wondered if she had embarrassed George by mentioning rum running.

It was only a short time after he had taken on Crew jobs along with his regular fishing route that George surprised Marie with what he called a Tin Lizzie. He had more money in his possession now than he had ever earned fishing year-round.

Marie only realized she was the owner of the Model T Ford when she went for her driving test. George nearly burst with joy when he saw her pleasure when accepting his gift.

"Like Granny said," he told her. "There's nothing stopping you women now."

Chapter Seven

Now that she was a landlubber, Marie and her Tin Lizzie cruised around the Cape, focusing on old homes by the sea and out in Hyannis Port. It was Granny Araujo who alerted her to the men who were knocking at the oldest houses in the neighborhood. Young families ignored them, sending them away. Properties owned by the elderly sat empty while families argued about possession or inheritance. If relatives died without wills or had been sent to state facilities for the infirm, occupancy was complicated. State auctions were becoming common, and properties were snatched up quickly by opportunists and developers.

Marie's routines changed, but she still attended church regularly and met with the women afterwards. They were ecstatic about her new car. News had spread quickly when she was learning to drive. But she rode her bicycle on the weekends. To Marie, good weather was meant for bicycling. The sea no longer called her to go fishing. Those days had passed, no longer in competition for her time.

In the women's group, there was a bit of competition to keep up with the news, be it local or national. Polly Allen stayed on top of everything. She spotted George teaching Marie to drive and predicted he would buy her a car. Devon remained levelheaded about Marie and George and always made it a point to work beside Marie.

While they sorted and put away silverware, Devon asked quietly, "Marie, do you miss him? You two were such buddies. Polly tells us you don't go out fishing anymore."

Marie answered with lowered eyes. "Of course I miss him. Any day we have bad weather; I drive by to be assured he's being careful and avoiding the storm. He spots me every time, and I tell him I simply want to let him know how much I enjoy the car. We both know I'm checking on him, and we get to laugh about it. But the sea now has him all to *herself*."

It was Polly who asked Marie directly if George's new partner was looking out for him. "I hear Bill Millett is up on things, carries a gun, and has made himself known up and down the shore. Sounds like he's a loyal, savvy partner."

Marie would only converse briefly when such questions were directed at her. "Bill is certainly trustworthy and has high regard for George. Bill's no sailor, though, so he's not always on George's boat."

***

Excitement in the group heightened in the spring when the church held its annual strawberry festival. It ran for a week and included craft tables, fish fries, games for children, and many tables set up with seating so that most people stayed all day. Visitors and tourists came as well. It was a great fundraiser for the church.

Shopkeepers like Devon, Bridget, and Polly donated their wares and their time. Marie spent a lot of time and donated muscle, too, setting up tents and booths, selling, and seeing that things ran smoothly. Men, including the fishermen—the rum runners, too—spent whole days at the festival, sampling special foods and looking for bargains. George spent a day assisting with set up.

"I miss going out to dinner with you, Marie," he said. "We can feast here today once the grills are fired up. This is wonderful! I must say, the Crew is demanding and doing extremely well by us. The competition is peaking. Since Bill doesn't need to fish, I have days not running rum, simply enjoying my favorite thing: catching bluefish or whatever else is running. Teaming up with Bill is so lucrative. I mean big payoffs. Fishing gives me relief from that competition stuff. I could use more days like this one. What do you say, let's save some Sundays to get together, for old times' sake?"

Marie did not hesitate to agree, and George kept his word all summer. Those were the times she heard about the arrests and wild goings on among the rum runners.

"Did I tell you about the Salvation Army guy walking across the Bourne Bridge?" he asked her at dinner one night. "Some of those armored trucks filled with expensive imports mistook him for an agent, tossed him a sack of money praying he wouldn't set the law on 'em. Poor bugger didn't know what hit him 'til he opened the sack! The mobsters were in such a hurry getting away, they never found out who he really was. Those armored trucks meet us right on the beach. Move so fast they're on and off before we even have a chance to anchor."

Nearly all the fishermen were using rock salt or

other devices to toss their liquor overboard whenever they saw officials in time. Some cases were never retrieved.

"One time, both the agents and our folks found crates of expensive French wines washed up on shore," George said. "Nobody asked any questions. Just took what they could carry and went on their way."

Many of George's stories were entertaining, yet they gave Marie the shivers when she realized how involved her friend was in the business. She noticed even George showed some emotion about the challenges that were arising.

"Marie, some of the fellows you know have had run ins with the law. Even though Howie doesn't own a boat, he's paid off Coast Guard men a few times to save the local fishermen their livelihoods."

Marie's anxiety increased when she heard about a skirmish, he himself had with a rival rum runner.

"How'd you hear about that?" he said with a frown. "It was more of a confrontation, anyway. I'm not one to get in a brawl. I will not put up with anyone trying to pirate my catch. Some darned fool thought my boat was full of expensive alcohol. Jumped aboard, gun in hand, demanding liquor. By the time he saw I only had fish, Bill had popped up out of nowhere and put an end to it."

"What do you mean, 'put an end to it'?" she asked.

"Well, I don't know who told you what, but Bill only fired one shot—and it was into the air. The jerk got the hell off my boat. So, who told you? Was what they said anywhere near what really happened?"

Marie had to admit that Polly Allen's story had been a bit exaggerated. "She heard a radio broadcast about a fisherman accosted by a rum runner," she said. "Bill was mentioned, but Polly knows you work together."

"Well, don't believe everything you hear." He chuckled, adding, "even things you see, like that Salvation Army guy getting that whopping bag of money. Those high-strung guys in the armored truck thought they'd pulled a fast one."

A long silence fell, confirming their mutual concern.

At another Sunday meeting, George and Marie planned to spread some joy by inviting their grandmothers to take a pleasure ride to Boston. Granny Araujo had expected to one day be invited to ride in the Tin Lizzie. George's grandmother, Laura Winters, was a bit hesitant.

"You really mean spend a whole day going out to Boston?" she asked George. "You already asked Marie's grandmother? What did she say?"

George had known the invitation would provoke more than one question from his father's mother. Laura Winter was still working hard on the farm. Her advanced age did not seem to have taken away her drive to pitch in and do more than her share of tasks. She was particularly devoted to the animals and took over the plowing or driving the mule cart whenever possible. In the spring, Laura was always the one to announce that it was time to tap the maple trees and to ready the cart to go to the grove. Few people could guess her actual age. She was tall and trim. Her gaunt face and high cheekbones revealed only a few wrinkles, mostly when she frowned. Her hair was usually wrapped snugly to fit under her hat. She was a taskmaster, still cooking for the large family and extra farmhands at harvest. Ordinary women's sizes were hard for her to find, and she sewed her own clothes, always simple, without vibrant colors or frills. Church and social events interfered with timely care of livestock and chickens, so she rarely attended.

"Well, Grandma, it might do you some good to enjoy a day away," George told her. "I hear tell Grandpa is weary of trying to get you to slow down. Granny Araujo would surely enjoy your company. She's all set to go. This weather is so balmy. Sunday would be a fine day, and Marie will pack a lunch for us. I promise to get you home before dark in time to collect the eggs."

Laura hid a smile. George was pleading with her just as he had when he was a kid, wanting to work alongside her in the horse barn. Back then, she always gave in.

"All right, if we get home before sundown, it might be an adventure. Is it true that you taught your girl to drive that machine?"

"We both drive, Grandma. I can teach you, too, if you're interested."

"Lord have mercy, George, you must be funning me." But her wry smile did not hide her genuine interest.

The route was mapped out, using byways and alternate roads off the beaten path. Marie fixed a large picnic lunch that could be nibbled at on the road and feasted on when they spotted a comfortable stop. Granny Araujo had chosen to wear her Sunday best. Laura wore a red coat she had made from flannel wool. Her matching red hat sat jauntily on her salt and pepper hair, loosely wrapped in a large bun.

"Can you slow down a bit, Marie?" Granny Araujo pleaded. "I brought my Kodak. Mrs. Winter can help and choose what she'd like a photo of."

Marie obliged, and they stopped frequently along the rolling surfside and the dunes. Tussling with the wind brought much laughter and lasting memories with the help of the Kodak.

When the outing ended at dusk, both elder ladies accepted much needed assistance climbing out of the car. They made a date to share more time together. For each of them, the smiles lasted long after they were home.

"George," Marie asked a few weeks later. "Have you noticed when you chance by the Hollow how Granny Araujo's porch now has a small cluster of elders, your grandma included, sitting on the extra chairs? It warms my heart every time I see them when I make my courtesy calls on my folks."

***

As George and Bill Millett wove their schedules together to fit the Crew assignments, Marie abandoned fishing completely. She and Jenny Strong were deeply engrossed in the rapid buying and selling of both land and houses. Marie spent hours in the public library. The head librarian, Virginia Hull, asked her if she was studying to become a lawyer.

"Oh, no, Virgie," Marie answered. "It's real estate I need to know about. Deeds and the eminent domain thing. Some of the old homesteads by the sea are being snapped up. There are some shady deals being forced on our elderly."

Virginia raised an eyebrow. "You could fool me. You're even talking like a lawyer."

Marie had recently heard similar words from Bill Millett. He could not resist commenting on how savvy and smart she was. He asked, too, if she were a lawyer. He would brag about knowing her.

"She's the real thing, George," he told his friend. "Smart, beautiful, skilled at sea, and she obviously loves you. You got me wondering. Are you the kind of guy who, well, you know, who doesn't go for …?"

George scowled at him. "You think I'm a pansy?"

"No, oh no, George!" Bill said. "I don't get it, that's all. Before I would make any advances in her direction myself …" His voice trailed off. Crestfallen, he looked at George and stammered, "Forget it, George. It's none of my damned business, and don't worry. I won't be making any moves on Marie."

The "trade" became normalized, and Bill continued to team up with George, not fishing but on all Crew missions. George maintained his proud reputation as an excellent fishermen and catcher of blues. Bill was very skilled at making sure the deals with Killcarney were safe and guaranteed top profits. What he did not do was keep his word about not making any advances toward Marie.

George discovered Bill's dalliance on one of his now cherished outings with her. Their time together had become even more precious now that Marie worked year-round with Jenny. Their trips to Boston and even to New York increased and enhanced their real estate ventures.

"It's like old times, Marie," George told her. "I really enjoy our beach picnic days. Both of our lives have shifted with triple incomes. Bill and I have made hundreds of dollars in a single week of jobs with the Crew.

And I've seen your name in *The Barnstable Patriot* and *The Register.* 'Jenny Strong and Marie Araujo will find you the home you've been dreaming about...' What a great advertisement."

At first, Marie simply smiled in agreement. Then slowly, she asked, "George, have you and Bill ever had a reason to talk about us? He made an awkward advance in my direction a while back. Sort of implied he was breaking some sort of agreement he'd made with you."

George burst into laughter. "What? Why, that scoundrel! He'd just about made up his mind that I was one of those men who loved men instead of women. Because our love relationship is beyond romantic, he figured he would be the man who could woo you into a romance. Marie, what did he say to you?"

After a long pause, Marie raised her eyes, glistening with tears. "I wanted to confess how much I love you even though I know how much you love the sea. I am certain he now knows it is *you* I truly love."

George's eyes also filled with tears. The embrace that followed confirmed the depth of their mutual love.

Chapter Eight

With the church group, Marie never shared what she learned from George. It surprised her at times that Polly kept up with all the arrests and increased high jackings of loot from the fishermen. The looters were called pirates, lying in wait on ships and on shore to rob fishermen before they delivered their booze. Other conversations suited Marie more, such as the engagement and party celebrations before Hazel's daughter's wedding. Many of the women gave handmade gifts on both occasions. Not being one of the proud crafters, Marie gave lovely, often luxurious gifts she bought in New York. Fancy perfume was a big hit, and novelty hats with flowers and ribbons made all the women envious.

Sarah, Hazel's daughter, was a beautiful, happy bride. Her mother told the group how the groom had been so filled with love and emotion that tears flowed unabashedly when he spoke his vows. Hazel closed her eyes while describing how her new son-in-law had held her daughter's hands so gently. In that state of enchanted recollection, she remarked, "Why, I don't recall feeling so loved and happy at my own wedding. I found myself weeping. Yes, weeping with joy."

Marie found herself smiling, remembering how she

felt on an outing with George. It had been a while back, but the warmth enveloped her as if she were back there, on the beach with George. The conversation turned, and the clean-up had nearly finished when she suddenly remembered Bill Millett's bid for her exclusive attention. The women froze at the sound of her hysterical laughter.

"What just struck Marie?" Devon was the first to speak.

"Dear girl, whatever is wrong? That's a bitter laugh!"

"You can tell us; you know your word is safe here."

"I'm sorry, ladies," she answered. "It occurred to me how confused some people get about love and tears and joy."

They all took seats, confident that Marie would tell them what had provoked her strong reaction.

"Oh, it's that thing about men, how scrambled and confused we can all get about love, sex, and romance," she said. "George's rum running partner told me George was homosexual, and that he could 'fix' the problem for me himself. That bastard. He approached me as if I was some pathetic creature lusting for male attention. I hauled off and punched him right in his face! He stayed off the docks for a few days until his black eye faded and the swelling went down." She paused. "It frightened me that I could fly off the handle like that. My hand was swollen, too, for a bit. Good Lord, I haven't spoken to anyone about this. Please, keep it under wraps."

The ensuing chuckles were muted at first, but then the women shouted their approval. "Good for you! You make us proud, Marie!" The air of triumph lingered in the hall as the women strode out of the building.

The winter of 1923 was mischievous, sneaking in several mild days that teased the fruit trees, prompting their buds to stir. But a sharp change to freezing meant the harvest would be small or nonexistent. The peach farmers were estimating their losses. The church women noticed, too.

"That *Old Farmer's Almanac* wasn't a darn bit useful this year," Mary Helen lamented.

Caroline was more cheerful. "I sure enjoyed these balmy days. I was able to use my clotheslines for large laundry loads. On those quick freeze days, I had to scurry getting everything inside before it froze stiff. My azaleas got nipped, too. Might not have any blossoms this year."

Heads nodded as Bridget said, "That cold snap kept my customers at home. They kept the oven on baking and kept the stove busy making soups and stews from the vegetables that got half frozen in the root cellar. We were all eating ice cream during the week and then hot soup on the weekend."

"The newcomers figure this is ordinary. They come out in all kinds of weather, bundled up like Eskimos," said Devon as she described how the unusual weather pattern affected her business. "The Sears Roebuck catalog must have done some good business on the Cape. I never saw so many hoods and muffs and furs! Just the week before, they were showing off their lacy shawls and chiffon dresses."

"I don't miss the backbreaking shoveling I usually have to do to clear the sidewalk for my customers." Polly was also smiling as she claimed, "I have had a profitable season. With so many year-round folks, there's been no big lulls, waiting for summer tourists. I have kept my prices up, stable the whole year. February second was not a predictor of this uncommon weather. The groundhog did not see his shadow."

March was a pleasant surprise for everyone. George and Marie skipped their usual work schedules and spent an extra day at the beach. Crocuses, narcissus and forsythia had all burst their way into bloom. They met no resistance as the ground was not frozen. Tulips had no trouble popping up in gardens.

"Don't remember any winters like this one," George said. "Folks have changed right into summer clothes. Saw some adults along with children wading in the shallows on the beach." George was grinning at Marie. She caught a hint of a dreamy look in his eyes.

"Why, what's on your mind, Mr. Winter?"

"I hope you can guess. I'd like to make this our memorable year. Marie, would you? I mean, can you consider adding 'wife' to the many things you do?"

"George, you are serious. Why, I ..." She stopped. "I would be so ... honored."

"Glory be, I was afraid to ask. I couldn't take your answer for granted. I fished this whole winter season and have stashed away enough profit to be a full-time husband and a part-time fisherman!" With increasing excitement, he added, "You know about the best houses and property on the Cape and in Hyannis Port. You could pick out a house for us!"

Their eyes met in that special way where words are not needed. Tears glistened as their bodies blended tightly.

The weekend flew by, and Marie was walking on air

when she went back to work on Monday. She knew her Sunday women's group and the whole church community would be as happy as she. Jenny was the first to hear the details. Their entire conversation on the drive to New York that day revolved around Marie's thoughts and hopes.

"George made it his business to bundle his money," Marie told Jenny. "Neither he nor Bill uses the bank, but that's where George is going today. He is convinced that buying a house will require proof that he can pay for property. He is going to open an account, insisting that my name be on it."

But that day at the bank, the clerk gave George important information.

"Well, sir, she will have to come in and sign. We use signatures to validate accounts. That is a very large sum of money! Both of your savings?" George was a bit annoyed as the clerk suggested he return on Tuesday with Marie. "Then you can both sign, sir."

"No, I cannot do that," said George. "I'm taking my boat out tomorrow. I'm getting important business done today. Just write her name in and leave space for the signature. I know she's at work today. Probably in Boston or New York. This is important, sir. You're right; this is an accumulation of our hard work together. It has got to have both names! Let me speak to your boss."

"You should not be walking around with this amount of money on you. Print her name, I will leave space for her signature. Print yours and sign, too. Your money will be safe here 'til you both come in tomorrow, no, Wednesday. No later than that, though, right?" The clerk looked over his shoulder as if hoping his boss couldn't overhear. There was another bank in town that would gladly accept such a deposit.

"No later than Wednesday, sir," promised George. "I've got a list of things to do today, out early tomorrow. Wednesday it is."

Chapter Nine

George finished his errands, ending at the jewelers. Before sunrise on Tuesday morning, he drove by Marie's, but her car was not in sight.

"Darn! They must be doing business in New York, maybe stayed over like they do sometimes. I'll get going now, get back before midday, and then park at her place 'til she shows up."

The temperature was dropping, and many boats were getting an early start. Even while the sky remained overcast, an uncanny wind arose from the east. The glorious sunset the evening before had left the sailors unprepared for what came to pass: a blizzard, howling and roaring before noon. The rum runners were the first to make it to shore. Many were near the British ships, which took off, heading out to sea in an attempt to outrun the sudden blinding snow and wind. The fishermen who were further out made a desperate run for shore. George and Bill Millett weren't doing an assignment for the Crew, but Bill and Howard Sullivan were at the docks when the sky darkened, and the snow and sleet pounded against windows. Every sailor who made it back to the docks pitched in to help the next boat that appeared in the sheets of snow. They salvaged what they could, stayed bundled on the dock, taking breaks to warm up in the nearby tavern.

"Any of you fellows know if George Winter went out today?" Howie asked every fisherman whom he knew, and he knew all the locals. No one knew about George.

It was dark when the last of the boats were made fast at the docks. That last boat was the first who could answer the question. "George Winter? Yeah, he went out real early like me. He's not back?"

The fisherman went on to describe the frightening day. "The sun hadn't come up yet, but the temperature was dropping like a stone. Gray sky, weird easterly wind. We weren't out far. I tucked myself between those foreign ships. Hunkered down, praying all the while. The big ships hightailed it further out to sea. The off-shore rum runners with the rigged motors were guarding their stash and circled around me, wanting me to 'lighten my load' by tossing them my liquor. Damn fools! Harassing fishermen, didn't pay no mind to the blizzard. They must have run into such bad storms up Newfoundland. Fast boats, guns cocked, pirating."

***

Jenny and Marie left New York on Monday, ran into wind and rain-flooded roads halfway, and decided to stay the night at an inn. It was Tuesday about noon when they heard about the unseasonal blizzard that hit the Cape. Marie immediately worried about George's plans.

"I know he isn't working with Bill on a Crew assignment," she told Jenny.

Not finding him at his home on Tuesday evening sent her into a panic. Her landlady was the first to

51

inform her of the missing fishermen.

Wednesday came and went. The crocuses were still blooming in the quickly melting snow. Fishermen kept to the shore, standing alongside families that lingered, came, went, returned. On Thursday, the families stayed away, commiserating with each other.

The Sunday sermons across the Cape offered special prayers for "those among us who have lost someone at sea during the storm." Marie Araujo was at church. Her blank stare required no explanation. After the service, Devon took her by the arm and guided her into the church hall.

"I don't think I will be of much help today," she said. "I have not been able to sleep."

Mary Helen and Annie Sullivan simply wrapped their arms around her. "We went over to your place on Wednesday morning," Annie said. "Landlady said you hadn't been home since the blizzard."

Marie found a way to smile in appreciation. "Oh, I couldn't go home. I've been staying with my folks. They don't think I should go home after the service today. Want me back with them for a while."

Devon set places on a small table by the kitchen door, pulled up chairs for the three of them. The rest of the ladies carried out the usual tasks, moving diners away from the small group at the table. There was no banter. The silence was respectful.

Polly Allen broke the somber mood. "Marie, what are your plans for the rest of the day? Going back to your folks again tonight? I would be glad to accompany you to your place so you can pick up things you might be wanting or needing tomorrow. It's best that you don't spend a lot of time alone."

Mary Helen spoke up. "I know two other men who did not get back to shore. Want you to know Howie and my man were late getting set to go. Arrived as the first blast hit. Annie, why don't *you* go with Marie? Polly, that was good thinking on your part, but Howie can follow Marie and Annie to her place, then they can go home together. That will free Marie up, not being obliged to bring you home, Polly."

Marie stood silent as the women finalized their offer.

The following Monday was another unseasonably warm, breezy March day. Jenny had been to the Hollow, looking for Marie at her parents' house, only to learn that Marie had returned to her own place after church on Sunday.

Now she found Marie already outside of her house, briefcase in hand.

"And just where do you think you're going, woman?" Jenny asked her.

Marie burst into tears and got into her car. Jenny plunked herself right in beside her and began to cry, too. Time stood still.

"He's gone, Jenny! He's gone! *She* stole him from me. My worst fear!"

Jenny did not interrupt until Marie quieted. "Marie, try not to make any big decisions for a while. I know you've made a bid on the old Wallace place out in the Port. There's no need to move quickly. Give yourself some time."

"Jenny, you have *no* idea what decisions I need to make, and soon!"

"My dear, what do you mean? The house? You know that can wait."

"No, Jenny, no! When I got home from church yesterday, my landlady told me there was a man asking for me. He left a note with her to give to me. Said it was urgent. It was Bill Millett! When it comes to business, he and George are close. I mean ... they *were* close. They used to ...”

“Dear Marie, let’s go inside and just sit a while. We are *not* going to be doing any work today.”

“Jenny, I’m headed to the bank. Bill’s note said it was urgent that I meet with him today. *Today*, at the bank on Main Street. The note did not make sense to me, so I went right to Bill’s place for an explanation. Then I got in touch with Virginia Hull. Pleaded with her to go to the library and verify what Bill told me. She’s a wonderful woman and I can now say a darned good friend. She looked up the law Bill spoke of: how the bank will take possession of all of George’s deposit: thousands of dollars he put in the bank to buy our house!”

“All right, let’s go to the bank then.” Jenny was still puzzled, but she had no intention of leaving Marie’s side.

When the bank clerk looked up to see a well-dressed Bill Millett, accompanied by two serious young women, one with a briefcase, he frantically beckoned to his boss. Bill had already visited the bank, the day after the blizzard. George had confided in him about his plans to buy a house and suggested Bill might be wise to open an account himself. George had warned him, “There is no one in town who doesn’t know you have lots of money. You could be a target for those organized gangsters.”

It was at that first visit, when Bill told him George Winter had advised him to deposit his money at this bank, that the clerk had let slip information.

"Well, your friend gave you good advice, but he sure better get back here as he promised. We had to put a hold on his account. There's just so much time.... Ah, well, let's get busy and open *your* account."

Bill caught the inference and feared the bank could indeed take possession of George's money.

Now, the teller ignored Marie, looking relieved as his boss sauntered into the lobby. But the boss' attention was riveted on Bill, who had moved to the teller at the next desk.

"Sir, I opened an account and need information in hand about your interest rates on savings," Bill was saying to the young man. "Are there any other products you have that would allow me to diversify my savings? Can you give me printed material that describes how I can have a portion of my deposit set aside to grow?"

Both clerks now turned to their boss, and Bill did the same.

"Paul," the boss said to the first clerk. "Surely you can assist the young lady."

"It's a matter of a needed signature, sir."

"Paul, I see Miss Strong is with the young lady. I can assure you if it is a matter of a witness of identity, you can trust Miss Strong to help. She is well known to the bank and can surely expedite matters." He turned to Bill. "And you, sir? Mr.?"

With calm authority, Bill replied, "I am William Millett, a resident here in Hyannis. And your name?"

The boss cleared his throat and, matching Bill's tone, declared, "I am the bank manager here at Hyannis Savings and Loan. Morgan Wetherbee at your service. Won't you please accompany me to my office? I am certain I can give you the information you requested along with printed material explaining our services and fully satisfy your needs."

Paul, Marie's clerk, hurriedly produced the forms he had set aside for George, expecting his return. Marie and Jenny carefully read through the documents. Marie signed immediately. Both women managed to hide their amazement at the massive sum of money in the account: twenty thousand dollars.

"I would also like printed material concerning your rates of interest and other products I might be interested in," Marie said. "Do you have any handy or will I need to make an appointment with Mr. Wetherbee?" She stared boldly at the clerk as he moved quickly to gather material from the drawer behind him. He handed Marie her bankbook along with a small packet of printed flyers.

His smile was pained as he emitted a sigh. "It's a pleasure to do business with you, Miss Araujo."

Outside the bank, Jenny and Marie stared at each other. Once in the car, they broke into laughter tinged with hysteria.

"That was the most awkward, creepy exchange," Marie said. "I am sure Bill will have more to tell us when we meet again."

Jenny responded with a proposal. "Why don't we arrange a lunch together as soon as possible? We need to keep close tabs on Mr. Millett. He is shrewd, and I have a sense he is sincere and has transferred his friendship with George to you. Did you notice how he deliberately distracted your clerk, drawing attention away from the signature dilemma?"

"I sure did, and the slick way he handled the manager, too. If there was a time frame for the bank to take over the account, it is no longer an issue."

It was Jenny who took the initiative, arranging a time when she and Marie could meet with Bill for lunch. Two weeks went by before a suitable date worked for all, and they met at Jenny's home.

Bill was the first to arrive. He was in an animated state, telling Jenny about his new experience working for the Winter family at the farm, when Marie arrived.

"I'm missing something exciting!" she said. "Did I hear you say you're working at the farm?"

Bill turned to fully face her, displaying a huge smile. "Yes, you heard correctly. I am now a happy turnip farmer!" Jenny bid them all sit down in the living room. "I never enjoyed it as much when I was working my family's farm, but I was a young whippersnapper, trying to be a good son. George and I often spoke of how we as young people were happy to get away from farm work for a spell."

"When did all this happen, Bill?" Jenny's smile grew as big as his.

There was not a moment through the meal when Bill was less animated. Marie only joined the conversation when complimenting Jenny on the lunch. She herself had brought dessert, and she smiled as she served the brownies and whipped cream. There was a brief reminiscence about the encounter at the bank, and then Marie went silent as Jenny and Bill continued to chat.

"The Winter family has taken me in as one of their own," said Bill. "Their pride in doing things well is contagious. If there is a big hauling job, I can fill in, and if weather dictates, we hustle the harvest: sons, daughters, and even Grandma Winter pitches in."

"How is Grandma Winter faring these days?" asked Jenny. "I worry about the elders. This vigil has taken a toll on all of us. Marie, have you noticed a change in your Granny?"

There was a pause before Marie responded. "She avoids much conversation about the storm and the missing men," she said. "I guess she thinks she is being protective. I've noticed a few little changes."

There was another pause while both Jenny and Bill awaited more details. Bill filled the silence with a report about Grandma Winter's zeal at gathering maple sap. Her energy surprised folks, and her expertise was admired by all. Marie's reticence was respected, and Bill's animated comments appreciated. Jenny promised to plan another lunch if either would be willing to come again.

"Oh, yes, Jenny, count me in and I will be happy to bring dessert again," said Marie. "It's been a long while since I enjoyed baking, and I can promise a great strawberry dessert. The crop survived this wild, angry weather."

Bill seemed overjoyed with the idea and asked if it would be okay if he brought some wine.

Jenny shouted with glee, proclaiming, "Bill, you can bring whatever you like, and wine will be perfect!"

The next time Jenny and Marie worked together, Jenny could not resist sharing her thoughts about Bill and Marie. "You have an odd connection," she told her friend. "He can barely keep his eyes off you, always admiring and complimenting everything you say or do. And you, Marie, seem to pay him no mind, like you don't even hear the admiration nor hear the warmth in his voice. It puzzles me."

"What? Hm, I guess you might say we have a unique connection, through George. They are ... were close partners."

"But Marie, the way you ignore him would discourage ordinary men. Could you be feeling angry that he got George working near full-time rum running? I almost feel embarrassed at times when you appear so oblivious to his obvious admiration! Do you dislike him?"

"Oh, Jenny, that's a long story. I'm sure Bill understands. He and I had a meeting of the minds a long time ago. Please do not allow yourself to fret over the way we behave."

"To be honest with you, Marie, I think you make a good couple. He's no longer rum running: just a healthy, handsome farmer." Jenny laughed as she watched Marie roll her eyes and blush.

"Enough about Bill," Marie said. "You and Claire Holmes have these notions about me finding a suitable partner. I have absolutely no interest in men currently. You give me comfort and courage to remain a single woman, if that's my fate. Single women can enjoy life and support themselves well."

They both smiled in agreement.

***

Any time the three of them were together, Jenny still noticed the strange way Bill and Marie related to each other. At church luncheons, Claire Holmes was open about getting Marie to notice men.

"How long do you think it will take for you to get

over losing the love of your life?" she asked Marie. "You are much too young to settle for being an old maid. My brother, Ernest, took a liking to you first time he saw you helping at the Strawberry Festival. You've always been attractive to men. The local fellas know you and George are committed to each other. Ernest doesn't know the history, immediately quizzed me about your availability, got excited when I said you were still single but committed..."

April arrived with timely showers and wonderful sunshine. The weather remained glorious, and, to the delight of the orchard farmers, the peach trees burst into full bloom. Every tree and shrub rejuvenated, unharmed by the topsy turvy winter blasts. Even people who were grieving those lost at sea moved on in their sorrow: in spite of heartfelt pain, they had not lost their faith, and they no longer felt paralyzed. As the Pastor proclaimed, "Grief is the price of love, and we will remember our loved ones forever."

There was no list of the ones lost in the blizzard. The community knew of each one and sustained their support in individual, creative ways. In the church hall, the church women honored those lost. The hall was not only used for luncheons, but also served as a space for pageants, plays, and dances. Townspeople could rent the space for bridal showers or other celebrations. Devon took it upon herself to find an area that could be easily viewed by all. At one end was a small stage with a velvety curtain that stayed drawn when the stage wasn't needed.

"That's my spot!" Devon declared. She spent weeks embroidering a poem on a large piece of burlap. It was a timely act in recognition of those lost.

***

On Thursday, April 29th, a body washed up on the beach at Hyannis Port.

"They say it's George Winter." It was Polly, sharing again what she had heard on the news. "Of course, his family barely could identify him—it was mostly bones, but his hair and the shirt his grandma made left no doubt."

Marie had not entered the hall, but the women assumed she had already heard from the Winter family. Funeral plans were probably in progress. Devon showed the women her large, embroidered burlap, which she had stretched onto a wooden frame.

"I'll consult with Marie about where best to display this," she said. "I got the Pastor's approval."

In black embroidery, bordered with seashells in greens and blues, she had stitched a long poem:

Crossing the Bar

Sunset and evening star
And one clear call for me!
And may there be no moaning at the bar,
When I put out to sea.

But such a tide as moving seems asleep,
Too full for sound and foam,
When that which drew from out the boundless deep
Turns again home.

Twilight and evening bell,
And after that the dark!
And may there be no sadness of farewell,
When I embark;

For tho' from out our bourne of Time and Place
The flood may bear me far,
I hope to see my Pilot face to face
When I have crost the bar.

—Alfred Lord Tennyson

As Devon held it up, Marie entered with some of the fishermen's wives, Mary Helen Pinkness and Annie Sullivan.

"Why Devon, how? Did you? What an amazing piece of work!" As Mary Helen stood speechless, Annie stopped talking and moved closer to feel the embroidery. Marie silently mouthed the words as she read the poem. Each woman found a way to touch and read the artwork. There was no need for conversation about where to hang it. Marie assisted Devon in setting it on the stage as the group hustled to get the luncheon set up.

Marie confirmed that funeral arrangements were being made.

"It will be a closed casket, and of course the visits will be at the farm," she said. "The two days will follow the old way, sitting vigil with the un-embalmed body to ensure the person is truly dead. From home, he will be interred in the Oak Neck Cemetery. No funeral parlor nor church service in the plans that Grandma Winter shared with me."

The women set about figuring how they could be of help.

"Of course, those of us in the choir will get permission to do a prayer and sing a hymn or two. Even if you are not in the choir, we'll robe you up and you can join us." It was Bridget, the lead soprano, who was compelling the others to commit to joining. "We can even save a bit of time today to choose what we all know well and get in a little practice. I believe anyone who can talk can surely do a bit of singing."

Polly countered with, "I am not so sure about that, Bridget. Have you ever sat beside the Sullivans when Howie gets the spirit!?" That brought a big laugh. Almost anyone near him had to hope the next hymn would not be one of his favorites.

A week did not go by before arrangements were finalized. Previous funerals held in March were well attended by the community, but George's decaying body, his well-known big family, and all the families in the Hollow prompted a larger than usual turnout. The plain pine casket rested in the dining room, the biggest at the farm. On top was a large bouquet of store-bought roses; it was too early for any from the garden. The kitchen table was laden with a variety of foods that family, friends and relatives supplied in endless amounts.

"The old ones are taking it hard," said an observant neighbor, who encouraged them to sit a while. Grandma Winter never left her 'station' at the head of the casket. Her elaborate black silk dress, fancier than anything she had ever worn, was covered by a black lace shawl. Granny Araujo arrived both days, and her sorrow and weariness showed heavily. George's parents and siblings moved among the guests, offering appreciation to all who had come to pay their respects. Marie spent part of each day with the family, her expression fixed in a look like a puppy being scolded without knowing why. She did not shed a tear.

When Jenny was there, she overheard the gossip. "The guns and rivalry have gotten so bad, who knows, he may have been wounded while trying to get to shore." Another voice carried: "It was his clothes that confirmed it was him. Some say there were holes in his shirt. Could have been made by bullets."

Ricky Killcarney arrived and tried to console the family and Marie with a prolonged conversation about his own grief at the loss of one of his best employees.

"I'm sure you will miss his loyalty and good work!" Marie said with vehemence.

Jenny, standing nearby, moved closer, and Marie turned away from Killcarney to whisper to her friend. "Frankly, Jenny, I do blame how this whole grubby 'adventure' has put our fishermen in harm's way. If it's not the pirates and organized crime, it's the jail they face every time they work for that, that, phony!"

Men had supplied a corner table with alcohol of all sorts. Their conversations were about their work. George's father was talking with Bill about the farm. "So glad you are with us. You might be interested to know how big our endeavor has grown. We have increased our yield, improved our product, and expanded our market. We have George to thank for the newest equipment. That also helped to slow Grandma down. I do believe, if George had taught her to drive, we would be in trouble. She kept telling us she was going to take him up on an offer he once made." Both men could smile, remembering how George and his grandma had always got along.

"George and I sometimes talked about farming," Bill said.

"Oh yes, he told me you are a turnip farmer. Said your folks sold out the whole lot to real estate folks. You happy getting back into farming?" They both knew the question came out of fear for Bill's life if he continued rum running.

"Well, your son and I had serious conversations about me and the farm. He said your older sons were deep into diversifying and have made a successful 'hauling' business doing hauling. No pun intended."

"That is so true, and it left me shorthanded at times," George's father said. "You have become my best seller of turnips!"

"My plans can now include banking and investments. Farming is far more enjoyable than working on boats."

It was pleasant conversation at the house both days, and especially when the church women made their appearance. The mood almost became joyous. Bridget got everyone to join in a hymn sing by asking for requests from the mourners.

"We all know this one," she encouraged. "Come on and join us with *Amazing Grace*." Every voice was not in tune, but the choir led loudly with fervor.

"Thank you, ladies." Bridget was proud as punch back at the church hall. "Why we sang more hymns at the Winters than we do on Sunday mornings!"

Annie Sullivan agreed. "Bridget, you even got all the men out of the kitchen. I don't know if the 'spirits' inspired them or if it was a beautiful way to let loose some emotions.”

As she spoke, families began drifting in for lunch, her family among the first. Howie dashed right to Marie and enfolded her in a big tender hug. From across the hall, Bridget shouted, “Howard Sullivan, the surprise bass! You should be in the men’s choir!”

Startled, Howie blushed. His big smile that followed earned him a return hug and pat on the back from Marie. “We all know your favorite hymns, yet you knew ALL of them and truly made us proud. Bridget has a point. You might enjoy singing with the men.”

His talent had been noticed in the pubs, where men often spontaneously joined in shanties and popular songs.

“With direction from the choir master and a wee bit of training, Howie, we can *enjoy* that bass voice every Sunday,” Marie told him.

As summer drew near, conversations in the hall remained focused on the lost fishermen. It was the end of May when Polly raised the issue of the embroidery. As always, she was the reliable newscaster of all local events.

“Looking ahead to June when the Sunday school year ends as well as these meals, I’d like you and Devon to settle on a permanent place for the framed embroidery,” she told Marie. “With it propped up on the stage, folks have been admiring it and touching it. I’ve spoken to the sextant. He can do a good job securing it on the wall or any place you two choose.”

The comment focused the women’s attention on Marie.

She and Devon looked about the hall. It was Marie who decided. “With the Strawberry Festival coming up, this hall may be in use with booths," she said. "Rain will bring things in here. Up on the stage curtain would be a good place. People won't be able to touch it. Over time, it could get damaged. Anybody known to the church can rent the space. It could even be mysteriously 'removed.' Devon, what do you think?"

***

June burst forth with a bumper crop of strawberries. Early vacationers went out in the fields with the parishioners. Word about the coming festival multiplied their interest in attending. The weekend weather prediction was perfect.

The Strawberry Festival elevated everyone's mood. When Marie and Bill Millett met again for lunch at Jenny's house, the conversation was all about the weather prediction and the influx of year-round folk and early summer arrivals.

"So glad you both could make it!" Jenny's welcome was sincere and did not show the weeks of the communicating and preparation required. An entire year had passed since their first meeting together after the bank business.

"I brought dessert, like I promised," said Marie. "It's strawberry shortcake with vanilla ice cream instead of whipped cream. OK if I put the ice cream in your refrigerator?"

"Of course, silly. I am afraid you will find lots of room right in the ice chamber. I should fill the space with straw until my ice man comes. I think the festival order has delayed his usual delivery schedule. It's a go for tomorrow. Bill, has anyone approached you to lend a hand?"

"Seriously, Jenny, surely you know I volunteered and got talked into guarding money and making runs to and from the bank. It has been a challenge to keep the vendors supplied with change. These vacationers seem to love twenty-dollar bills."

"No, Bill, I hadn't heard. We've both been out of town, winding things up at work to be free to pitch in at the festival. I wonder what else we'll discover. What I do know is the Brinks Company would only contract for a day, and Sunday was never the day they agreed upon."

Marie busied herself adding silverware to the table, along with dessert dishes she knew where to find.

"Annie Sullivan's husband, Howie, recruited me," Bill said. "He is aware and has some notion I am handy with a gun. Howie said the daily money exchanges have been challenging, and there are many more folks carrying guns. Big crowds attract bad actors and clever pickpockets, too. There is lots of rum business money exchanging hands and people are purchasing lavishly. Folks in the booths have raised their prices to keep up with the times."

"Enough about money and guns, let's eat. The lasagna won't stay warm while we're jabbering."

There were oohs and ahs about the delicious hot rolls and crisp salad. Jenny had managed to keep the house cool in June while she was baking, and her guests were very appreciative. While they savored Bill's after-dinner wine, Bill addressed Marie like a big brother. "The feuding Wallace brothers have been up to no good. Marie, check the bidding process closely. Young Harry has given up hope of inheriting and the conniving oldest son is trying desperately to maneuver a 'private' sale without the authority's awareness. I spent several days at the bank doing business and eavesdropped on a conversation. Neither of the men were paying attention to me. If you would like, I will go with you to the authorities. The presence of a male figure makes a difference when dealing with officials. That house will always have special meaning even if you never occupy it."

"Why, thanks for that information, Bill. I will surely get in touch with you after I contact them today." That is exactly what she did once the meal and brief tidying up were finished.

Chapter Ten

Claire and her brother, Ernest Bearse, both worked at the hardware store.

She kept Marie updated about Ernest. "The owners have opened a second shop to accommodate the increased sales in lumber and siding," Claire told her. "Ernest works in the new shop and has become used to having dinner with us."

And she made sure her brother knew about Marie.

"Sis, it used to annoy me at first, but now it makes me curious," Ernest said. "So, Marie is buying a house? I am not even looking for female companionship. What I am interested in is a flat of my own. Every place is now so expensive. Even seasonal renting has become lucrative. A place I saw empty this spring stayed empty. When I checked with the family, they said it's now a summer rental. They can afford to let it lay empty from Thanksgiving until Memorial Day. I need a place of my own. Being in the military affects guys in different ways. I'm looking to meet up with some of my veteran buddies. That's why I want a place of my own: to meet with our group. We've spread out up and down the East Coast, but there's a few fellows in town and we're inviting the gang here to the Strawberry Festival. Later, we plan a weekend with a good old clambake. Some of them have sweethearts or had girlfriends before joining up, but we do not plan on having women when we meet up. It's kinda like you and your church group, good company, no complicated heartbreaks or rejections. Just a good feeling being together, shootin' the breeze. What is it about your friend Marie that has you church women so focused on her? Aren't there plenty of other single women around town these days? I noticed many of my high school buddies, both the guys and the women, have left the Cape for job opportunities as near as Malden and as far away as New York. Summer people are as thick as flies, already in solid groups."

Ernest had to grin when he added, "Not that I've been looking."

Strawberry Festival

Once everything was set up, the crowds filled the churchyard and abutting field. Marie spotted Bill. He was again dressed impeccably and walked about with authority; gun holstered in plain view.

"Why, you're looking like an official security guard," she said to him.

"I don't want to be wearing a uniform."

Marie was pleased that they could both laugh and get on with their tasks. Their meeting with the officials had ended well. Hers was the final bid, and things were moving toward finality. As for Ernest, their introduction seemed to be elusive. Claire Holmes lost track of her brother in the hustle and bustle and Ernest went about testing his intuition, trying to see if he could spot this mysterious Marie.

As the day ended, Marie felt a bit melancholy, remembering how she and George made their commitment to save weekends for each other. Bill noticed her pensive expression and dared to put his arm around her, giving her a light hug and a smile as he spoke earnestly. "I miss him, too, dear girl. I guess there will always be times and places when we have our good old memories bubble up." He released her as quickly as he had tucked her under his arm, and they were again able to smile and get on with their final tasks.

Ernest noticed them, concluded they were a handsome couple and went home believing he would probably never find this myth of a woman.

Chapter Eleven

The Court House and County Deeds Office clarified and made current the necessary papers. Marie was now the proud owner of the Wallace estate: "house, land, and all structures there on." She had taken Bill up on his offer to accompany her and they left the office with a hand full of keys, proceeded to the locksmith and went to her property. Once there, they were not aware their every move was being observed.

With relief and gratitude, when every door and shed had been attended to, Marie asked Bill to join her when she did a walkthrough with Jenny, Howard, and Annie Sullivan.

Bill made certain Jenny, Annie, and Howard knew Marie wanted them to do the inspection with her. A time was not specified, but Bill graciously and with forethought, chose not to join. He wanted to step back, give Marie her space, and avoid any confusion. He didn't want her to misinterpret his support; he knew she was perfectly capable of handling her own affairs.

Early the very next morning, Marie deliberately drove out alone. Appreciative of her friends' support and interest, she yearned to do her first complete inspection in solitude. She was surprised and a bit leery when she saw a figure, standing in her doorway.

A man.

The Estate

The Sullivans and Jenny planned to go to Marie's, drive to the estate together and perhaps have dinner afterwards. They all arrived at her flat by noon only to find Marie's car was not there. They waited a while, wondering if they had misunderstood the details of the invitation. They all heard from Marie the same day she and Bill left the locksmith.

The group left for Hyannis Port. They cheered at the sight of Marie's car. Jenny rapped boldly with the brass knocker on the huge wooden door. Marie did not appear. Howie went off to check the grounds. Annie crowded Jenny at the door, her pale face distorted in panic.

"What's the matter, Annie? You look like you've seen a ghost."

"There is something amiss here, Jenny. I don't like it a bit. Howie's gone poking around the grounds. There are lots of buildings back there; maybe a barn, horse stall, outhouse. Too many shrubs and trees and Lord only knows what else! Something's not right. Why didn't she wait for us?"

They were both startled to hear men's voices.

"Bill told us he wouldn't be here." Without hesitation, Jenny shouted in a commanding voice, "Who goes there?!"

Howard strolled around to the front of the house with a strange older man with sad, pale blue eyes, a big frown, and shaggy grey hair.

"This feller is Buster Shattuck, he is the Wallace's

groundskeeper. Says Marie is up there checking the chimney and gazing at the ocean. He sure knows a lot about the place, inside and out. Says there's a flush indoor toilet." Howie was excited as a child, ready to give more details, when Annie shouted, "Shut up, Howard! How can we get to that place where Marie is?"

"Take it easy, Annie. She's fine. Of course, she was a bit startled by Mr. Shattuck waiting to show her around, but I think he is anxious to work for her."

Buster Shattuck stood silent when Annie took off, hurled her body against the big door and disappeared.

"Oh my, she's madder than a hornet. Jenny, please check on her. She's about ready to bust a gut!"

The women could be heard calling to each other. Annie located the stairs to the walkway by the chimney.

"Over here, Jenny, to the stairs. Marie, are you OK?" Completely out of breath, she puffed, "What are you doing here?" Bustling along the walkway, Annie found Marie with tears sliding down her sunlit face.

"What can I do? Why the tears?"

When Jenny arrived, Marie was smiling. "Up here gazing at all this land: the trees, the ocean. Ladies, it is magnificent. I could stay here all day."

Annie was quietly crying. "Marie, you're frightening me. You left without us. There's that grizzly gardener acting like he's supposed to be here, and Howie, all friendly with him and unconcerned. I have got a bad feeling. Talk to me. What are you trying to do?"

"So sorry, Annie, I did not mean to worry you or anybody else. I wanted to do it alone, to get a feeling of the place." Almost in a whisper, she added, "My place, Annie."

Jenny stood by as Annie wrapped her arms around

Marie. Both wept some more before speaking. "I honestly came up here to inspect the chimney," Marie said. "No need for wood fires right now, but old chimneys have burned down houses. When I sell homes like this, I have the mason check for cracks, for lining or caulking problems. This one is in good condition: no debris, or cracks."

Jenny, still observing, quietly asked, "Marie, what about the groundskeeper, hanging around?"

"Oh, Jenny, he gave me a fright this morning. I had no idea who was at my door so early in the morning. He explained himself. Been watching from afar and up close. He saw us change the locks on the sheds where he keeps all his tools. He anticipated we would be here early and planned to cut down the overgrowth and shrubs, which he proceeded to do after I gave him the key. One large key opens all the sheds. I kept my distance by having him test out the new locks.

He went right to work whacking down the brush. I think he was just as nervous and skittery as I was."

"You going to hire him? Pay him to continue tending the grounds?" Jenny asked in her serious, professional voice.

"Until I actually occupy the place, I think it will be a good investment." The three women moved carefully down the stairs to the lower level of the house. Annie was still blustering as they went into the big entry hall.

"Howard, are you still so enchanted with that old man that you forgot we came here to help Marie? It's all right, Annie. We are all here. Now let's see what work lies ahead for Marie." Jenny remained calm and serious, while Marie managed a smile. She was totally at ease as she directed them from the front entry. "There are six bedrooms ..."

"Oh, Marie, wait a minute," Howie said. "Buster is outside, wanting to return the shed key."

The groundskeeper came into the entryway. "I have not been in here since the last time the Misses paid me. Things seem to be in decent condition."

Jenny took the key and handed it to Marie. Then she gave the man a stern look as she dug in her purse and produced a pencil and a piece of paper. "Mr. Shattuck, please write your whereabouts so Miss Araujo can contact you."

Buster prattled on as he took pains to write his information. "Those boys come and go as they please, take things, even when the parents were both alive. They ruled the roost. Parents taught them good manners, but they turned out to be pretty headstrong." He covered his mouth with his hand, grinned at Jenny as he gave her the paper. "Shouldn't be in people's business."

Both he and Howard recognized he had been dismissed. "No mind, Buster, we understand," Howard said. "You have known these folks for years."

It was Annie's loud sigh and big grin that allowed the tension to melt away. Marie also smiled as she continued the tour. "The bedrooms are pretty much intact: no linen. The brothers have obviously gone through every room, removing what pleased them, no signs of vandalism nor anything in disrepair. They left all the large pieces of furniture and even left every utensil imaginable in the pantry off the summer kitchen!"

They passed the large kitchen and laundry room before mounting the stairs. "Looks like the big job is going to be sweeping and dusting." Jenny was lagging, nosing into every nook and cranny. "Windows, too. So many, clouded with grit and dust!"

"And all the drapes up here need to be replaced. I found signs of mice in that big pantry, but there's no food there. Must have been coming in during winters to nest." Marie continued her stroll, noticing the women had stopped at the sight of the water closet in the hallway.

Howard had dropped out on the first floor. He shouted to Annie, "Come back down and see the big bathroom off the dining area. Now this is a treasure!"

Jenny, nearest to him, came down first. "Looks like the ones Marie and I have seen in New York and in Boston hotels. All this splendor is perfectly ordinary in lovely houses like this."

"I didn't know I lost you two downstairs," Marie was laughing. "Annie is still in the toilet up here. Isn't it wonderful: flush toilets. I will need to locate the cesspool and leach field. The outhouse is still functional: well-maintained, mulch, sweet lime, and toilet paper! OK, folks, why not set about exploring on your own. Then we can gather in the kitchen by dinner time."

That is what they did, wandering inside and out. Howard was excited about the carriage house and animal stockade he had previously discovered while walking about with Buster. He took over the outdoor tour, identifying old garden plots, flowering shrubs, and estate boundary lines.

As the sun began to set, they were surprised to find Marie in the kitchen, spreading out a large array of food. Barely taking a moment to stop talking about the amazing things they found in and on the estate, they devoured the hearty meal with gusto.

Summer

In the summer, the after-church luncheon was downgraded to "Coffee Hour" until September. Fewer people remained after the service, and half who came were summer vacationers. Bridget O'Toole found her scones were the best advertisement for her bakery. The compliments flew and she declared, "Oh, come on over to the bakery. Boston cream pie is my best seller in summer, but surely you can find *your* favorite. I am easy to find: 13 Main Street." Her directions were simple to follow in relation to the church.

Polly Allen specialized in making the strong black coffee with fresh cream. Hot or cold, it was a favorite. Those who were not coffee lovers would take her up on the offer, "There's tea and lemonade right over here." The homemakers did their baking the night before and provided a variety of cookies and frosted cupcakes. Everyone left refreshed and pleased. Marie was not one of the regular bakers and often missed days when she had appointments selling and showing homes to folks who sought her out. Word-of-mouth from satisfied customers often made Sunday the best day to meet.

Polly Allen, the newspaper enthusiast, shared troubling news on a day when Marie was absent. "The Sheriff has been keeping his eye on Damon, the oldest Wallace boy. He has been lingering in saloons some weekends, full of angry talk complaining how young Harry caused them to lose the money from the sale of the estate. He is threatening some kind of vengeance!"

"What can he legally do?" Devon asked in a worried

voice. "Doesn't he have a family and a business to run in upper New York State?"

"Maybe his business isn't doing so well, and he needs money." Others chimed in with concern. "Does Marie know about this? If it is in the news, she must have some idea."

With authority, Polly explained, "The newspaper described him as a drunkard, whining about women taking over and his brothers betraying him. They would have locked him up overnight to sober up if he wasn't rich. He may be feeling guilty not signing the property over to young Harry."

Clean up took no time at all and the group dispersed, still speculating how this could affect Marie.

It was one of Marie's contractors who told her about the drunken Wallace man, drifting around the saloons. "His wife may have kicked him out when this heavy drinking started. I haven't seen him, but heard the Sheriff did not intend to let him become a nuisance. Read him the riot act and promised to lock him up if he shows up again in that condition."

Marie listened closely and mentioned the conversation to Bill when they met by chance at the bank.

"Marie, do you have a timeline for moving into your property?" he asked "I know you have a team doing cleanup work inside, and Buster Shattuck is on site daily. No brush or ugly trees hide the house from view. It stands out like the jewel that it really is."

"My thinking right now is to not occupy it by myself but treat it like a modest bed and breakfast: cheaper than a short hotel stay and a place where my prospective customers can stay overnight while I show them places further down the Cape. I am not too keen on making breakfast for folks, but could keep it simple, or allow them to stir up simple meals for themselves. Working in that kitchen is a treat. It has every gadget and kitchen tool imaginable."

"That is a splendid idea, Marie, and please do not hesitate to call on me for any kind of assistance. You may not know this, but I hope to demonstrate one day that I am a very good cook."

She hadn't paid much attention to the newspaper reports before hearing from others about the drunkenness. Now her vigilance was heightened. She made certain she accompanied her helpers no matter if they were family, friends or for hire and scrutinized the news for further mention of the Wallace men.

The following Sunday, Marie was with the church group at coffee hour. "Have I told you about my bed and breakfast idea? The thought came in my head when I spruced up those six lovely bedrooms. For a wild and crazy moment, I thought about having my folks move in with me. My mom has been having a wonderful time joining me shopping for linens and curtains and such. I was relieved when she made it clear she would never, ever live in a place like *this* place and she believed I only bought it to put it on the market and make 'tons of money.' She was horrified when I told her I intended to live in it."

"Well, I was horrified, too, when I heard about that Damen Wallace making wild threats of vengeance, drunk and loitering around town a couple of weekends ago. Maybe you should think twice about rattling around a place big as that." Polly was sincere and the first to refer to safety issues.

Others were slow to comment, but Devon quietly

asked, "Is there something I could help with, Marie? Are you keeping your old flat and spending time out there when you take in lodgers? It's so exciting. I am willing to join your cleaning crew for free. I would love to see the place and help you out."

It was the opening Claire was waiting for, "Are you moving out of your old place? Ernest is still hankering to get out of our parents' house and be on his own again. Before joining the service, he shared a flat with two of his buddies. Both married before the war ended and that flat is rented to tourists now. It's unbelievable how much rentals now charge. And people are more than willing to pay. You haven't met Ernest yet since he's become such an old man veteran." She laughed at describing her kid brother as an old man. "He keeps wanting to only socialize with other veterans and they hang out sharing war stories and such. Serious, loud conversations Mom and Dad worry about. It's like he is on a rescue mission, rounding up buddies who are struggling a bit to adjust to civilian life. They don't even need to drink to get rowdy. They don't go to the taverns, and they eat more food in one evening than you can imagine."

Mary Helen added, "I sure wish my nephew would get out and about. He's not the same. My sister brought him to Boston to the VA hospital, she got so worried at first. They told her it was normal for soldiers who saw combat to take a while to adjust. Are you worried about Ernest?"

"No, not at all. He's the same busybody, the funny, imaginative kid he always was. But a lot more serious and focused. The service seemed to make him grow up fast. The big change for him is that guys from town he grew up with have moved away and the others have married, busy with raising families and earning money. He spends a lot of time with me and my hubby, because Mark likes listening to his war stories."

"Did he see the fighting, the horror like my nephew? I sure would not want to listen to that stuff," Mary Helen asked.

"Well, Ernie was a medic. Got a lot of training and he talks about the amazing things the doctors and nurses did in the field tents. For a while I believe he was thinking about training to be a nurse. Figured doctor or surgeon training would be too challenging."

"Maybe he chooses not to talk about the worst parts, too sad. Working with doctors he surely saw awful things. My nephew has nightmares, wakes up reliving the gunfire, shouting, and frightening my sister."

"I'm so sorry, Mary Helen. What did they do to help him at the Vets' hospital?"

"Oh, they seemed to think that in time, he will get past the worst of it. They acted like it was not unusual and we shouldn't worry about it."

Claire looked so sad, Devon changed the subject by again asking Marie when she might come and help her. Hearing Devon's interest and feeling that she had abandoned her church friends, Marie came up with an idea.

"Ladies, by the end of September, I will surely have the place in order, and you and your families can come to a housewarming. I am thinking about calling it the Greet and Meet Bed and Breakfast, the exclusive G&M B&B."

Only Mary Helen, sitting next to her, heard Polly say, "Ugh huh, the George and Marie."

Chapter Twelve

It was still August when Marie invited Granny and Laura Winter to see the finished work at the house. She felt comfortable alerting Bill of her plans. She invited him to go out and see the refrigerator that had been reactivated. He warned her about some of the early types that ran on toxic gasses and convinced her to consult with the company identified on the equipment.

"Bill, I made an extra key for you, so you won't have to wait for me to go along when you look at it. So far, it has been working well, and a service man from the company met with me and Jenny to get it running. He left instructions along with a safety guarantee."

At Bill's and Jenny's urging, she made a formal working contract with Buster but still felt better going to the property with others.

"Buster has taken to carrying that shot gun whenever he is on the property," she told them. "He hasn't forgotten about the drunken Wallace fellow. I've noticed that at night more and more cars and even trucks come down this road. New houses have gone up since the sewer line was extended and the paved road attracts vacationers."

"Do tell Buster I have a key," Bill said. "I do not want to be the first person he shoots. With summer nearly over, it will be dark earlier. How often do you work out there after dark? Does Buster's contract include all seven days and evenings, too?"

"You ask good questions, Bill. I'm not sure I have all the answers. Some evenings I meet with people I am selling to. The library at the house is now my official office and my trade card has the map to show how to find me. I go to my flat at night to sleep and agreed to allow Mr. Shattuck to set up a 'resting' place in the carriage house. It has a wide, open front, but good shelter. He is not paid for 24 hours but I suspect he sometimes stays there overnight. It's probably not a strict contract, but it does make me feel safe when he's around. He has been doing this on his own for years. Sunday is his day off and he seems to honor that. My parents have been spending Sunday afternoons with me at the house. We do not see him when we are there."

"I do not intend to go to your place at night, but if you have worries that he is overstepping his bounds, you let me know at once. Will you, please?"

Marie smiled. "I do believe you have become the big brother that I never had. Yes, Bill, I will keep you up to date on the happenings at the G&M B&B."

"Does that mean I can tag along when you invite the grandmothers?" he asked. "I would really enjoy that. I would meet you on the property so the ladies will fit nicely in your Tin Lizzie."

"How nice of you to offer," Marie said. "I have been relying heavily on Jenny. She might want to join too and yet not feel obligated if she has other business, knowing you will be there. I will find a day they both agree to and see if it works for you."

***

Neither grandmother hesitated to accept Marie's invitation, planned for the following Saturday. Bill checked the refrigerator beforehand and put staples in both the tiny ice box and the large new one.[2] Wine, cheese, and fresh fruit along with a potato salad he knew would surprise Marie. She would surely bring fresh bread, milk, and a sweet dessert.

On their arrival, Granny Araujo was the first to shout, "Why, this road is paved, and look, there's the ocean. And all that land."

Laura Winter spotted the barn and outhouses dotting the property. "Is that a stall back there? Marie, do you have a mule? I can see a cart."

The tires crackled as they turned off the paved road. The drive was packed solid with clam, quahog, and other seashells, saved from decades of beach trips and homemade chowders and embedded purposely into the damp soil to prevent tracking mud into the home. Solid as the surface had become, the sound was an announcement that someone in a heavy vehicle had arrived.

Laura, still scouring the landscape, exclaimed, "Why, that's an old animal stockade, as well as the two sheds on the corners. You say the folks who owned this place were carpenters? Well, nothing back there seems rundown. Looks like they could be put to good use."

"I considered tearing them down, but both Jenny and I figure they can be converted to interesting adventures for the children of guests I'm hoping to attract,"

---

[2]In the 1920s, refrigerators in catalogs were fancy ice boxes.

Marie said. "In October, all the hotels let their extra help go and close sections of their buildings. My customers will welcome reasonably priced lodgings for a brief stay, avoiding those expensive, fancy hotels on Main Street. It is beautiful out here."

They could see Bill coming towards them from the front yard and, behind him, Granny saw Buster. "My land, could that be Lem Shattuck's oldest son they call Buster? Those eyes ... but he seems too old to be the kid I remember."

It was Buster who hurried over to assist Granny out of the car. "Why, Miss Araujo, how wonderful to see you. Careful now, the drive is rough until we get out front."

Laura scowled and, not very discreetly, asked Marie, "Who is that shaggy old man with Mr. Millett? He lives near here?"

"No, no, Mother Winter, he is the old groundskeeper for the Wallace family who built this place. I've hired him to continue the good work he has done, even after the place was abandoned while the heirs fought each other about ownership. He keeps the grounds immaculate."

"Well, he sure could use a good cleaning up. Could have lice in that long shaggy, unkempt hair and beard." She held her gaze on him, making it clear she did not require his assistance.

"Ladies, we can tour the grounds after we freshen up and have a spot of tea." Marie was anxious for them to see the grand entry with the electric chandelier, no candles, and the water closet in the hallway.

Granny Araujo barged ahead, leading Buster to the nearest outbuilding. "Now is this a laundry shed? There could be an old well in there with a working pump. Everything looks so well cared for, except you. Your mother would be embarrassed to see you looking so disheveled."

His sad eyes brightened as he attempted to focus Granny's attention away from the laundry shed. "Yes, Granny, that's the laundry shed, pump still works, and I can rebuild the lines for drying outside if the Missus would like. You'll be pleased to know there are water closets in the house with flush toilets." He was like a kid again, excited to show off a place he loved and dreamed about owning.

"Don't you dare come in this fancy house until you've cleaned yourself up. Tame that hair and crop that awful beard. You are a Shattuck, and you can be proud of that good name!" She all but shoved him away from the house. He never stopped beaming at her as he obediently walked towards the laundry shed.

Inside, the ladies greeted Bill, already arrived, and there was laughter and exclaiming over the beauty of Marie's new home.

"This is more elegant than any house I have ever seen." Granny Araujo was animated and bursting with comments.

Carrying herself with her usual dignity, Laura Winter gently ran her hands over the furniture. "I sure wish you had your Kodak with you today," she said quietly to Granny. "Such beauty, so well restored or preserved. Marie, you bought all this. How did you manage? It must have cost...."

Before she could finish, Marie burst into tears, wrapped her arms around Laura and whispered. "George, Mother Winters. George put all his money along with mine. *He* chose this to be our home."

Laura grasped Marie tightly and whispered, "Oh dear, oh dear, I should have known. Please forgive me."

Granny spoke right up. "Nothing to forgive, Laura, I was wondering the same thing. It's like a dream, this place, shared by two people we love. I can feel the love within this place. It will be the best, most beautiful bed and breakfast ever, and that love will never die."

It was a while before anyone spoke. Bill, his eyes as moist as everyone else, gave a big sigh and suggested everyone sit a spell, then decide what they wanted to see next before they sat down to eat. He had sneaked a casserole into the oven and went to check on it.

Marie, in a rather dazed state, followed Bill and asked him, "When did you get here today? You have something in my oven? I have some food prepared, too."

"I know, I checked your ice box." His smile was contagious. The two grandmothers nodded and gave each other sly glances that Marie caught.

"OK, you two, don't be getting any wild notions. Bill and I have a sister, brotherly friendship, and that is all it is intended to be."

The ground floor tour ended, and the elders declined to tackle the stairs. Granny promised Laura she would get some Kodak photos of the bedrooms from Marie and share them.

"Comfort food, ladies," Bill announced. "My own recipe for macaroni and cheese with the best butter crumb topping you have ever tasted. It will go well with Marie's fresh vegetables and Bridget's Bakers Dozen, crusty French bread. The chicken is warm and there is something in that little refrigerator to top it all off. Wine anyone?"

Leftovers were parceled into take-home dishes and the kitchen was clean before evening fell. As they prepared for the drive home, a loud knocking on the front door caught everyone's attention.

"It's Buster. I just know it's Buster." Granny spoke with excitement at the prospect. "If he really cleaned up, is it all right with you, Marie, if we give him a plate of leftovers? I bet he has not had a good homecooked meal since his young wife died in childbirth, twenty years ago."

"What? Why, Granny, you know all this about that raggedy old man? Twenty years ago? Oh, my." For the first time, Laura allowed herself to feel a bit of sympathy for the man and his sad history.

"Oh, that explains a lot about Buster," Marie said. "Here I thought he was a bachelor whose family turned away from him. Granny, are his parents dead, too?"

Bill went to the door as the women stood, questioning Granny. "Oh, my, yes. He cared for them until they died. They were a prominent family, the Shattucks. When they died, he gave up the farm, sold the livestock except for the donkey. We bought the cow, then the young man devoted himself to the old folks here."

Bill stopped the conversation by escorting Buster right into the dining room. He was cleanshaven, in shabby but clean overalls, and wore a bright red plaid shirt. His grey hair was pulled back into a loose ponytail, beard gone. His bright smile made his odd blue eyes sparkle.

"Just wanted to offer my services if you ladies wanted a tour of the grounds before dark."

He stopped as he noticed they were prepared to leave. Granny nearly tumbled over, reaching to give him a big hug.

"Not today, dear boy, but would you like a take-home dish of leftovers? A token of appreciation for your offer. Marie, do you want me to fix the plate? Maybe you can choose a plate he can return later."

Laura had already headed for the kitchen. The three women combined their own plates into a basket before Bill could say a word.

As Marie drove the grandmothers home, she heard Laura tell Granny, "I sure do wish you had brought that Kodak. No one would believe that raggedy old man could spruce up to look so wonderful. You have always had a way with young ones, Miss Araujo. Today you turned that old man back into a boy."

Chapter Thirteen

Marie was ready to complete her plan for an open house where church folks and other special guests could enjoy a sunny autumn day at the B&B. She took photos for the grandmothers and included "Guest Rooms" in her newspaper advertisement.

The weekly luncheons had resumed in the church hall, and Marie found it easy to share news about progress at the B&B. Their pastor had made a point to visit and bless the estate, main house, buildings and grounds.

"Do I need to make up a broadside invitation for my open house, or will it get too much attention from folks I don't expect or intend to welcome?" She was serious, trusting the women would offer good advice.

"You don't want Ricky Killcarney to show up," Polly interjected with an exaggerated ugly face. "You surely want Pastor Walker, since he has ceremoniously blessed your property without needing to be invited."

Devon was taking Marie's request for suggestions seriously. "No broadcast, Marie. Word of mouth and a notice in the Parish Bulletin. Everyone else, like Virginia in the library, should get special, personal invitations. I'll be glad to help write them out. Let's help Marie make her list."

Claire worried at the thought of someone like Ricky showing up and asked, "Marie, are you living out there now? Or are you keeping your flat and you're only working at the estate?"

Polly Allen jumped in with a plausible solution. "You could have Claire's brother as your first year-round guest, Marie. He could be on the property constantly, then that old groundskeeper could be dismissed. He's such an odd fellow, lurking around constantly. Ernest has been hoping to rent your old flat, right, Claire?"

"Oh, Polly, I appreciate your concern," Marie said. "Jenny helped me draw up a contract with Mr. Shattuck, a job offer. If he is to be on the property as groundskeeper, that will mean no weekends and no evenings. I've told him that since it is now a bed and breakfast, he will be working regular hours. His services will have limits. It's obvious he loves the place and has been caring for it without compensation."

Polly's frown remained while Claire beamed with delight. "Oh Polly, what a grand idea. Ernest would surely be a good year-round lodger."

"I bet that friend of George's would do the same thing and pay plenty of rent in addition to managing," Devon said. "I think he has hopes of protecting you or watching out for you, ever since you both lost George."

Marie looked quizzical. "Humph, you all have more creative and imaginative ideas than me or my parents. Such thoughts have not crossed my mind. I am still investigating the legal steps I must take to make the estate a business: the permits, inspections, and everything it needs to bring back the original beauty."

The women continued to exchange ideas for Marie

as they began closing up the hall until next Sunday's coffee hour.

Sales Women

Jenny specialized in land, and if a potential customer was interested in buying a home, she sent them to Marie. One afternoon, she came out to the estate, expecting to find Marie at her office.

The first thing Marie shared as she warmly greeted Jenny was the conversation she had had with the church women.

"You did take the first step already by formalizing Buster's role," Jenny said. "And there's no doubt Bill would jump at the opportunity to help out. But those ideas need some serious thought. Do you even know this Ernest fellow? He was a kid when he left for the military."

They were walking together when they saw Buster behind the main house near the old animal stockade. He had the shot gun slung by his side.

"He still has a key to the outbuildings?" Jenny asked.

"Yes, I had one made for him. All the groundskeeping tools are stored there. He knows there will be limits and a salary forthcoming."

He saw them and immediately headed over. "I knew it. My days here are going to be cut short." His sad tone matched his posture. "You here to fire me today? You both look serious."

"Buster, no!" Marie said. "We've talked about the written agreement. I sent a copy with the mailman. Didn't you receive it? I should have handed it to you and gone over it with you, but I haven't seen you until today. Why are you carrying the shot gun?"

"Oh, oh that. Just checking all the sheds, making sure no one can hide away out here. Boarded up the window in the old laundry shed. A person could just about live there: water well, wood stove and all. Not been used for years, but that Damon, that drunken son of a gun, he knows every inch of this place and used to have rowdy teen parties out here. Might be where he got his first liking for liquor. He can't be trusted."

Buster started to walk away as Marie called out, "I can meet you here tomorrow afternoon, so we can look at the job agreement and salary."

Without turning around, he lumbered off, raising his voice in response, "Yes Ma'am."

"There hasn't been any gossip about those Wallace boys for a good while," Jenny said. "I don't think you have to worry about the drunkard. The whole town is on the lookout for any return foolishness from any of them." She was confidant as she spoke, but Marie was disturbed by the sight of the shot gun and reminder of the drinking incident.

"Maybe I should think more seriously about Devon and Polly's ideas." They continued a thorough survey of the sheds, stalls, and deserted outhouse.

"They are all sturdy," Marie said as they finished. "Tearing them down would be one option, but I would rather think of ways to make them useful and secure. Any thoughts, Jenny?"

"Abandoned outhouse, laundry shed, carriage house, abandoned animal stalls. It's almost a children's adventure playground. The carriage house is on one level and, with the doors wide open, a safe playhouse.

The animal stall is way back there. Not sure what use it would be unless you want to keep a donkey. The old cart is in excellent condition. Buster probably still uses it. There's fresh manure out there. Does he own a mule and use a cart to police the open acres?"

Without waiting for an answer, Jenny kept imagining uses for the buildings they had scrutinized. "Now that laundry shed. I wonder if Buster had considered living out there. He's not an easy one to figure out. Loyal, that's for certain. Odd, no doubt about that. Where does he actually live right now? I had him write down his address, but the lane he listed was unfamiliar to me. It must be nearby or adjacent to this acreage. Do you know?"

"He walks home from here," Marie said. "I've never noticed a road, but the only paved road is in front of the house. When they ran city water down to the new properties and mandated cesspools to protect the beaches, they paved the old trails. *You* know there are many roadways here with grass growing in the middle. When George and I took our grandmothers on a picnic, we searched out the old byways near the beaches. They get plenty of use year-round: names like Burrough' s Lane and Cabbott's Landing. Buster's address is 10 Shelby Lane. A conversation with the mailman I've met at the house will clear that up for me."

They went into the library office to finalize the business opportunities Jenny had brought.

***

The end of spring brought an unexpected crowd of beach lovers to the Greet & Meet Bed & Breakfast.

Weekends, Marie was both hosting and hustling: showing properties and expediting sales and rentals. The
overload emboldened her to reach out to Bill Millett and
take him up on his offer to help.

"Morning, Marie. Any empty rooms this weekend?
I'm free both Saturday and Sunday once the crop is
planted. I can spell you from kitchen duty while you get
your paperwork done and you can get to your Sunday
services, too. The farm respects the Sabbath. Only the
animals get any attention. Grandma Laura sees to that.
The rest of us tidy up loose ends, put our feet up or
bodies down and rest." His broad smile convinced
Marie that he was already committed to cook and clean
for her and her guests two days in a row.

"Well, you certainly proved yourself a special asset
to us. Guests raved about your French toast. That first
Sunday you pitched in initiated rave reviews that
brought a couple of new customers. I'm offering them a
staple of eggs, boiled or scrambled, a variety of breads,
toast, and sometimes a surprise offer of hot biscuits
with local jams and jellies. The menu is simple, always
fresh fruit, or juices, good robust coffee, tea and cocoa.
The pantry is full and available for snacks. Few people
use the peanut butter, but if Granny sends cookies,
those disappear. I considered adding bacon and sausage, but recently a Jewish family surprised me by
commenting how wonderful our breakfast was. They
only ate kosher and avoided hotels in Hyannis after an
incident with a hotel chef."

"No problem, Marie. Your summer kitchen can be
the designated cook and serve area for pork products. I
can bring bacon and sausage and even keep it separat-
ed in the ice box out there. You are so wise and

thoughtful, Marie. Jewish families, I never would have...”

As he paused, Marie was quick to respond. “Give yourself credit, Bill. Your few voluntary step-in days as host put this place in the top ratings.”

He ended their conversation by heading to the summer kitchen to set up the special kosher cooking and storage area.

***

“I've got some good news. Devon, you will be surprised. I took Bill Millett up on his offer to cook for me at the B&B.” Marie's eyes glistened in girlish delight as Devon stopped moving about to hear above the clatter of dishes as they cleaned up after Sunday services.

“It made such a wonderful difference having a male host,” Marie continued. “Guests raved to me about how gracious he was and the deliciousness of his French toast. Bill was there for a couple of Saturdays last month, when it started getting so busy, and by the next weekend, a new boarder told me a friend sent her to my place because of the amazing chef. I may not have to advertise in the paper for a spell. So many guests are making early reservations. I'd hate to turn anyone away because we were booked full.”

Polly was smiling with pleasure and approval. “Did you all hear that? She said ‘we.’ Bill has become a partner by default. We are so happy for you. That adventure and daring in you has made your dream a reality.”

Devon stared at Polly to assure herself there was no rivalry or sarcasm in the complement. Assured, she said, “Marie you definitely will not need to advertise.

Two of my regular customers have asked how many guests you can accommodate. They have relatives who weekend on the Cape and would love to avoid downtown hotels and enjoy a B&B out in the Port with a nearby uncrowded beach."

Mary Helen moved closer. "Oh, Marie, I've been thinking about your grandmother and George's too. Have they been able to visit again? The place looks so beautiful this spring. You've added that hedge of flowering rhododendron and daffodils and tulips along the driveway. We drove by after church last week. Is that the work of the old groundskeeper? You were not sure if you wanted or needed him around, acting like he was policing the place."

"Now that's an amazing thing, Mary Helen." All work came to a halt as Marie rose so everyone could hear her answer.

"First, your question about the grandmothers. My Granny is not faring very well. She is not able to move about easily. Arthritis, rheumatism, some combination has made it hard for her to climb stairs or walk much without pain. But she has been in charge of the beautification of the grounds. Buster, the Wallace family's old groundskeeper, has become attached to Granny. He visits with her; she makes suggestions about which shrubs and flowers do best and which blossom all year. It's a beautiful, kind of melancholy rekindled relationship. She remembers him from childhood and knew his parents. George's Grandmother gets over to Granny's, too, and together they think about ways to improve the property. Grandma Winter drew a plan on paper showing how easily I can make a safe play space for children in the carriage house. It's amazing. They have been so involved and helpful after that first and only visit."

Marie was taking a deep breath, ready to finish her account, when Annie Sullivan shouted, "Now this is our old Marie! You've got me so excited and wanting to get back out there and work on the grounds or the play area. There are so many possibilities. And seeing you so happy." Tears welled in Annie's eyes as she dashed over and gave Marie a warm hug. A group hurrah rang out in the hall. Smiles and some tears accompanied the completion of the tasks.

***

Summer arrived quickly and plans for the Strawberry Festival once more became the focus of conversation in the hall.

"I promise, I'll make sure you get to meet my brother Ernest this year," Claire told Marie. "He's doing some carpentering now for the hardware store. I'll get a team together, and we'll get that play area done for you before the festival."

The weather was perfect for the festival, more like mid-summer than early June. Preparations were well underway, and the attendance was bound to be the best the church had seen in years.

Ernie made sure he helped wherever Marie was pitching in. She noticed and was amused.

"Ah, here's that happy face again. You certainly seem to be enjoying whatever you are doing. Wounded soldiers were fortunate to witness that comforting smile of yours."

Ernest's heart leaped, pleased and surprised she remembered the conversation from their first formal meeting at her place. Claire had brought her entire family to the estate right before the festival began. She arrived with her husband, Mark, daughter, Ruth, and brother, a wagon load of lumber, borrowed tools, and Laura Winter's drawing. Grandma Winter had sent the drawing and supply list to Claire at her job. On arrival, Claire announced, "That fat envelope that Mrs. Winter gave me also had money in it, so I didn't waste any time rounding up our team. Glad you're here today, Marie. I apologize for not giving you a time we could begin the project. Ran into Bill, he said he was coming to help today. Feared you might be on a business venture in town. Please, if I can interrupt whatever you're doing. Take a look at these plans and let me know if we can actually start today. We can always come back at your convenience once we unload."

Without hesitation, Marie bid them to begin and went over the plans while giving directions.

"Oh, that's a perfect place for a swing. Leave the lumber inside the carriage house. This beautiful weather can't last forever, and we could use a little rain."

Buster quickly joined them, looking like he knew what was going on.

Bill spoke up and gathered folks together. "Happy to meet everybody. Let me do some introductions."

Mark, daughter Ruth, and Ernest were the only ones who had not met Buster, and the introductions turned into lively conversations. Mark bragged about his brother-in-law's military service. Even as they began hammering and sawing, conversation never stopped. Ruth was anxious to talk with Bill about why he no longer worked for Ricky. Her rum runner friend was talking about marriage.

She admitted to Bill, "I can't bear the thought of marrying a rum runner. Mr. Millett, did you stop working for the Crew because of the danger? I do know how brave you are. George never carried a gun like some other fishermen. He was much safer when you two worked together."

"Why, all the fishermen know about danger; the profits are the attraction. I suggest you have a heart-to-heart talk with your special friend and perhaps make an agreement about what amount of money he would want to make. The danger wasn't what made me leave the Crew, Ruth. I made enough money to start investing. Try having a serious conversation with him. Worry won't bring about change." She smiled at the honest answer from someone she'd barely met.

Ernest ended the conversation, telling his niece, "Rum running has some aspects of war. Neither is worth dying for. Guns put everyone in danger. Friendly fire and collateral damage let the military dismiss the reckless loss of life. That's why I refused to carry a gun."

Marie and Claire listened and rarely interrupted.

Mark was quick to get in the conversation, a bit anxious about his daughter's possible marriage. "Ernie, didn't you say going into the military was one good option for a young man like Ruth's beau?"

"Only the commissioned officers make any kind of money in the military, Mark. I was a CO, but that only meant I wouldn't carry a gun."

Claire asked Ernest to explain or expand on one of his military ventures she was familiar with. "Tell Marie what a CO is. You and those fellows are the real heroes."

"Sis, because we never carried guns doesn't mean we were not trained to use them."

In that one productive day, everyone pitching in learned the difference between a Commanding Officer and a Conscientious Objector and how duties differed for men of color. Ernest was an entertaining storyteller. He made his duties sound so interesting he was asked to say more.

"A hospital in a tent? Now how big was the tent? Really, surgery too?" It was Buster and Marie who interrupted, requesting more details. Both Claire and Mark were quick to expand if Ernest was busy doing something complicated with tools.

Ernest had some questions, too, but they were asked quietly and specifically to Bill.

"Marie is such an amazing person," Ernie said. "It's not often that you meet a young lady with her ingenuity and curiosity. Bill, you seem very close and special to her. You two considering partnership beyond business? I am hesitant to try and get to know her better. My sister Claire has been egging me on ever since I got out of the service."

"No way, Ernie," Bill tried to muffle his laughter as he quietly clarified his closeness to Marie as that of a dear friend. No romance ever. "We have been clear and honest with each other," he said. "She's certainly worth making a bid for but watch out. She's got some strong feelings about independence. No man will ever boss her."

It was a very memorable day. The entire group did not assemble again, but individually came out to add the finishing touches, painting, hanging the swings, polishing and cleaning up. All was completed before the rain came and the festival began.

***

Autumn came quickly and Marie's invitations resulted in a large turnout of families. Children of church members mingled with children of bed & breakfast guests. They ran about exploring the play area and settled in small groups in the shade of the carriage house. Adults stood near the refreshment tables or sat in chairs borrowed from church and on loan from the funeral parlor. Ernest, with his sister, niece and brother-in-law, took over the roasting of hot dogs and refilling the never-ending bowl of alcohol-free punch. Marie's church group women did not ask what she would like assistance with but simply came with families in tow and went about setting up, filling up, and acting as hosts. Greeting people, mingling and introducing folks was a job Bill took on once he got a nodding approval from Marie. The smorgasbord of sandwiches, roasted corn, and crudité allowed people to walk about and converse.

Buster was the one who first saw the small plume of smoke. When he spotted a figure running towards the road, he fired a round in the air. Bill, hearing a gunshot, ran towards the sound, pistol in hand. He shouted to Buster and was relieved to see him stow the shot gun and grab a bucket of water from the laundry shed.

"Grandmother Winter, where are you going?" Marie and the guests stood motionless. Laura Winter was the only woman running towards the smoke. As she began pumping water into every vessel in the shed, men ran to join Bill and Buster, effectively dousing the grass fire

104

that was roaring towards the old outhouse. Howie, heading towards the road, saw an automobile racing down the road.

"I'm heading to town to get the fire brigade," he shouted. In moments, he was gone. Women gathered up the children and stood near enough to see how efficiently the men set up a chain to bring the water to a large, smoldering black patch near the outbuildings.

"Buster, whatever is happening back there? Are you all right? What got your attention before we saw the smoke?" Marie was breathless from fright.

By the time the Brigade arrived there were no flames coming from the stockade, where the grassy land ended. Had the old brambles and brush not been removed; the outbuildings would have been fully engulfed. The fire chief was informed about the running figure while his men doused the grass to steam and soaked the nearby structures for prevention. Damon Wallace was the prime suspect, and the constable was notified. Buster did not speak with the fire chief or the police.

Bill addressed the guests.

"Everything is under control. Please feel free to make the best of this event, allow the children to finish their games so they don't go home frightened."

Marie encouraged guests to take home desserts, which were plentiful. "I have baskets from Devon's shop that we fancied we'd be using for Easter basket fun. I'll fetch them."

People did leave early but not hastily.

"We'll be here until sundown, Marie." Polly Allen made the commitment without consulting the other women.

"Yes, yes, that's a wise decision, Polly. We certainly will."

It was Damon's drunken boasting the next evening that resulted in his arrest.

"That female bitch who stole my property, I showed her a thing or two. I burned the place down!"

The invited guests who had attended that day had vivid tales to share with townsfolk. The popularity of the Greet & Meet Bread & Breakfast increased ten-fold. There was not a weekend all winter that Marie did not have guests.

Chapter Fourteen

It wasn't long after spring burst once more into full bloom that Howard, Annie's husband, noticed a familiar figure down on the wharf. After a few sightings, he wandered close enough to confirm. It was Marie.

"Why, it *is* you, Marie. You look like you're ready to join the fleet. It's wonderful to see you in work clothes, rough pants, warm jacket and all, ready to go out to sea. Come aboard, girl. You're always welcome. It will do you good to haul in a few pounds of fish. Honestly, dear girl, I think a heartfelt urge brings you down here."

"Oh, I've come down before on balmy mornings, to take in the sights and smells." Her voice trailed off as she met Howie's welcoming gaze.

"I'm hauling with the Marcott brothers, only Jim going out today. That's why I'm joining him. You'd be more than welcome. Make a full crew of three. Hey, Jim! Guess who might be joining us today? Marie!"

"Whoa, Howie, you're really putting me to the test. Maybe my heart brings me down here but my head, thankfully, is keeping me honest. I'm not sure I could even be helpful, I mean good at, I mean if I should..."

As she paused, a big grin lit up her face when Howie reached out to her to climb in behind him. There was a misty haze lifting off the water in the shallows by the dock. It quickly disappeared with the rising sun as the Marcott boat left the shore. Marie's spirit rose as well, as the third member of a successful day's catch.

At the end of that Saturday venture, Marie felt a reminiscent weariness that allowed her to ignore paperwork, enjoy a bowl of hot chowder, crusty bread and hot black tea. There were other Saturday morning fishing trips that followed. Howard would make the invitation by presenting the day and time when they met at church.

It was after the next successful Strawberry Festival and a summer coffee hour that Ernest offered Marie a different invitation.

"Hello, Marie. I want to catch you before you hop on that bicycle. Claire has badgered me to attend church, claiming the summer services are shorter and the coffee hour is the best. It's not easy for me to hide my feelings, and I'm hoping you know how happy I am to have met you. Sis and Mark and I have spent many a Sunday at your place while you worked in the library or were off with customers. I feel like I've been your guest. Will you let me host you at Claire's today? Sis, Larry and Ruth are heading for Marconi Beach. The surfers there put on quite a show. The dunes are great, too. They'll be in Wellfleet until sundown. I'm still bunking in with my parents, so Claire makes their place available often. I'm looking to gather my Vets' group at their house, too, so the group won't bother my folks every month."

"Your Vets' group? Now I learned a great deal about your troop but Veterans' group? How many of you gather? You're the leader?" They were outdoors by the bike rack when she noticed there were more bicycles there than usual. "You came on bike today? Oh, of course, Claire and Larry will be heading down to Wellfleet."

Flustered, Marie paused and composed herself. "Sorry, Ernest, for asking so many questions. It's not like me to pry into people's business. The day you all teamed up to create the play area, the conversation kept moving along so fast, I barely had opportunity to ask the questions that kept popping up in my head. I think all of us were glad to meet one another and curious, too."

"That was a very special day. Please, ask me all the questions you'd like. I sometimes talk too much, so feel free to slow me down." They were both silent while churchgoers came, hopped on their bikes and peddled away. Ernest broke the silence, still gazing at Marie and smiling.

"Well, can you, will you join me today? I made a picnic lunch. Coffee hour is substantial but not very nutritious."

"Well, I really hadn't planned to do much at all today. Yesterday I did a bit of fishing with Howie and his buddies. It mellows me out, so I get to honor the Sabbath, as Granny would say. Going on a picnic sounds pretty relaxing. Did you really make the lunch, or is this your sister's plan?"

"Give me a little credit, Marie. I am perfectly capable of making a lunch. But I will say, Claire thought it was the smartest idea I ever had." His infectious smile prompted Marie to return a smile as they mounted their bikes and headed to Clair's, then down Sea Street to the beach.

***

109

Marie and Ernest found themselves waving happily as they passed friends and acquaintances along the way. One stranger turned to wave at them, two young adults enjoying a bike ride, minding the drifts of sand along the gutters.

"It's getting warm enough to swim. I've built up a sweat."

"No bathing today, Ernie. Not prepared." The bantering continued until Marie chose a grassy knoll with a good view of the surf.

"Oh, my, how tightly you rolled that big old quilt. Do your parents know of its whereabouts?"

"It is big and old. It's been used many times as a beach blanket. No sand in the salad today. Oh, do you want the menu before it's spread out?"

"Oh, no. No, no... yes, I do. And I want to help empty the basket." She grabbed the napkin-wrapped bundles of silverware. Ernest grabbed her hands.

"You have bruises and callouses on both hands. This bruise is fresh and very red. When did this happen?"

"Oh, I went fishing yesterday. That fresh bruise will heal quickly with one hot salt water soak. I heal easily. I was moving a little too fast, not cautious. That squall in the late afternoon sent us hurrying to shore prematurely."

He kept a gentle grip on both hands, inspecting them closely.

"Please, Ernest, I mean it. The skin's not even broken."

"You're forgetting I have seen small injuries like this fester. Tetanus is not unusual in bruises that happen outdoors and on boats."

"That's the medic in you, Ernie. This is no war injury. It's just red."

He had to smile at his exaggerated concern. His worry had come from past experience in horrid circumstances. She blushed and both laughed as they emptied the basket together.

"I must say your potato salad is kind of different. German? You mixed everything together while the potatoes were still hot? Mm, a touch of apple cider vinegar?"

"You're a good culinary detective. Can you believe I baked the bread, too? In our household growing up, I was not spared kitchen duty, and my dad is still the best chef in the house. He got me curious and interested in bread making before I was school age. The yeast process and kneading fascinated me. Claire is a fancy baker. Not like Bridget, but I mean fancy cakes and varieties of cookies."

"The mayonnaise in the chicken salad is delicious. Did you ...?"

"Oh no, that's store bought."

When they savored the chocolate-covered strawberries, Marie stopped the inquisition and simply relished the novelty. The afternoon sun dictated their move to a more shaded spot, nearer to the road under a sapling tree. There they sat at a picnic table with attached bench. Several families had arrived, and their children were running barefoot in the small eddies of water that appeared when the tide went out.

"My, I would wade in the freshwater ponds, but the sea is still a bit too cold for me. It will even be warmer in October than it is right now."

"Let's face it Ernie, those daring surfers down Wellfleet wear tight rubber bodysuits year-round."

Long comfortable silences completed the day. Shoes came off. Marie, who discreetly rolled down her hose, only tucked them in her shoes when they peddled their way back.

That evening, she relaxed at home just as she had after fishing the previous day.

The rest of the Hays family were at home when Ernest arrived. Surprised to see them, he questioned, "You abandoned the surfer extravaganza? No good waves today?"

"It was a good show, but very crowded and it got very hot. We couldn't find any shade except in a picnic area near the parking lot. We caught the breeze, enjoyed our lunch and met some interesting folks who had come all the way from Boston. How did it go with you and Marie?"

Mark and Ruth busied themselves stowing away the beach and picnic paraphernalia, while Claire gave Ernest a hand washing the few dishes and silverware in his basket.

"It was really nice, Sis. She's good company. Light-hearted and fun."

"Did you tell her you got accepted at the nurses' training school?"

"No, but I made a fool of myself checking a bruise on her hand. She has hands like old sailors: callouses and scars."

"Well, she was a fisherman-woman for years with George and years before that. She left home real young and that was the only job she ever had until she met up with Jenny Strong."

"I think I may have embarrassed her, noticing how rough her hands are, and she had an angry red bruise.

No bandage protection."

"Nurse Bearse, perhaps you should carry bandages with you on your next date."

"Next date? Now Sis, let's not rush things here. It feels good to be building a friendship. I'm not taking anything for granted. I do want to ask her about using that big summer kitchen for our veterans' meetings. Wish I had brought it up. I've spent a lot of time at her place, finishing the seesaw and swings, stowing things and cleaning up. Buster Shattuck gave me a tour of the whole place, inside and out. He called to her in her office, asked if he could show somebody around the rental area. She hollered back, OK. That was it. There's a spectacular view of the beach from the staircase and chimney landing. Guess tourists call it the 'widow's walk.' Railing goes all around to the front of the house. You have a chance to explore the whole place?"

"No, some of the ladies went out when the grandmothers toured. I've been outside and in the kitchens and big pantry. I've seen the walkway. It enhances the mansion, adds charm. How is it that you never mentioned it to Marie, that you've been accepted at that prestigious nursing training school in Worcester? You were so pleased and excited to be admitted with other young men. Weren't some of them veterans, too? You said you'd be living there. A first step to leaving the folks' house."

"Worcester is only a couple of hours away by car. The train goes into Boston, and I'm sure there's a stop in Worcester or a transfer. I'll be getting more details before September. That's when I'll begin living at the hospital or nearby for three years. The women live in a dormitory, but since there are fewer men, we will be in quarters in town. Doctors, the interns, live in flats above the main hospital. It's all kind of new to me so I have not announced anything to people. I hope you and Mark are not spreading the word. It's not a secret, but there's a lot more details I want to know. One reason I'm so pleased you two welcomed the veterans to meet here. They know there's a change coming up in the fall."

"You're pretty ambitious now. Who will take over your group? Now I see why asking Marie about the big summer kitchen will be amazing."

"Sis, right now I've become the convener and host of the group. You've met the regulars. Most of them are older and wiser than me, served for longer stints. We share information and guide each other to special help and resources, but what makes it attractive is the fellowship. That camaraderie we all feel the loss of once we muster out. It's a brotherhood, and when you add food, cards and other games, the group adds joy and melts away the urge to shy away from social life. A visit to Boston VA hospital to get information and apply for benefits inspired me to share real good information to the vets in the Hollow. I knew and they knew a few fellows who were 'lost' and hiding away. From that small bunch of about a half-dozen, word spread. The horror stories and nightmares fade away. We can even joke around about the night terrors and the times we flinch at loud noises."

"Well, I've heard Mom and Dad remark how rowdy it can get, but they are very impressed and notice how quickly and well you all tidy up and refrain from smoking indoors. No alcohol abuse, either."

"Well, if or when I ask Marie about meeting once a

month in that big summer kitchen, I'd also like to invite Mark to stick with us. He has been wonderful, dropping in and appreciating the stuff we now feel safe to own up to. He's a darn good card player, too when we're short a set of four."

"Did I hear my name? Ruth and I have been eavesdropping. I'm wanting to know more about the nursing program for men. I thought men went to the asylums to train. Me, part of the veterans' group? Now that's an invitation I can't refuse. Ernie, I knew many of those fellows before the war. It's a miracle to see how that kind of shy few have become so outgoing and full of fun!"

"Oh, I'm just rambling on here. There's not much change coming up this summer, but it would be a dream come true to if the group could have a clambake at the B&B on the Fourth of July."

The following Sunday, before the meal in the church hall, Ernest did not hesitate to seek Marie out and reach for her hands. Startled, she pulled away, then placed her hands on her cheeks and laughed.

"Ernest Bearse, are you checking up on me? Really. You will be surprised to see I am not only completely healed, but I've been using lanolin to soften the calluses." Voluntarily, she stretched out her hands for inspection.

Women brushed by them, leaving the sanctuary before the recessional hymn to set up the lunch. Ernest held her hands close to him to give the hurrying women room. Like kids in the schoolyard, they giggled their way into the serving area. Marie handed him the jug of cream while she lined up several small crystal creamers. They both ignored the questioning, curious glances from the other workers. Devon was the first to comment.

"We have a new volunteer!"

"No, no," Ernest protested. "I'm simply an eager, early patron."

No one stopped working and Ernest pitched in so skillfully, there was no pause before other parishioners and guests filed into the hall. Howard immediately grabbed hold of Ernest, greeting him warmly.

"You beat us all today. You make the coffee?"

A din of chatter erupted so Ernest could only respond with a negative shake of the head. New faces received special attention and an orientation, while the regular attendees greeted each other with pleasantries and good humor. Everything moved along per usual, with the exception of Ernie's getting the lion's share of attention, especially from Polly and Devon. Marie beamed while she greeted new people and regulars.

Ernest inched away from his inquisitors to whisper to Marie. "You abandoned me, help!" She grabbed his hand and led him behind the roll top wooden screen that hid the sink and work area. Empty vessels, platters and mugs were quickly piling up on the counter.

"You're such a good sport, I bet we'll get out of here early if you and I get a head start washing these dishes."

"That sounds like an invitation with a challenge. Where's the tea towels? You wash and I dry or vice versa?"

"You're washing! I'm protecting my hands." No one heard their laughter, but Devon came bursting through the gate entry at the end of the long counter and joined them in the merriment. She quickly placed the clean, dried dishes in their proper places.

They did finish the clean up early and gave Ernest a round of applause.

Polly pronounced, "Well, Marie, I see you have a new buddy in addition to your Big Brother."

There was a palpable hush as people looked to each other for reactions. The babble normalized as they all shared appreciations and farewells along with broad smiles. Marie was among the last to gather her things along with a big sack. Ernest tagged behind, offering to carry the bag.

"You taking all the tea towels and tablecloths with you? No biking today. You have your car."

Not relinquishing the bag, she answered, "Yes, I have my Tin Lizzie. You want a ride? Got your bike, or riding home with the other Holmes folks?"

He followed her like a devoted pup. "No matter how I got here, I'd like to ride with you." And he did.

"Were you embarrassed when Polly, as usual, took the liberty to speak her mind? You feel alright about being my 'buddy?' "

"I sure don't have any other claim on you. To be honest, I would very much like to be or to mean a lot more to you, but there's a lot we don't know about each other."

"Well, my 'business' is more public than most people. What is it that you don't know about me, Mr. Bearse?"

"I know you're easy to get along with and real good company. Somehow, I wasn't thinking of you as a career sailor, full-time fisherman: your life before selling land and houses. I do know you were young when you left your parents' home. You surely understand why I am suffocating, living back home after being on my own and serving in the military. Even with a good job and increased salary, I have imposed on Claire and Mark for breathing space. I am sounding like an ungrateful son, but I really think you do understand." They rode along silently for a while, then Ernest continued.

"I haven't stopped looking for a place worth the high prices they are demanding. It's true, I want to believe I know more about you than I've been able to share about myself. I'm sure you have noticed how I try to be in places where you are. Even when you are working in your library, I have been nearby."

"What!? You in my house? "

"No. Not often. Only when the gang worked on the play area and at the open house."

"You've been watching me in my house? That feels creepy. I mean, that's unnerving, I mean, I feel exposed."

Distracted, Marie had driven them to her home. Not attempting to hide her frustration and ire, she raised her hands and proclaimed, "Oh my. I can get you to your sister' s or wherever you need to go. By any chance is your bicycle at church?" Marie's face was as red as a poppy, teary-eyed as she tried to cover her face. Ernest reached for her hands as they wiped away the errant tears. She relented, allowing him to pull her into his arms as she cried.

"I am truly embarrassed, and I honestly don't know much about you, Ernest." She eased away in an attempt to compose herself. "It's not that I don't care. I don't want to be confusing. I mean, causing you to feel I want more from you than a friendship. You are so easy to be with, and you know how to have fun. You're lighthearted, and I like you a lot."

She sat bolt upright, pulled a tea towel out of the sack to wipe away her tears and then blow her nose.

"Oh my, Mr. Bearse, I do want to know more about you."

Ernest confessed, "I have been hesitant sharing hopes and thoughts with you. I regret that and will make amends. My bike is not at the church. Claire and Mark saw I had a ride with you. Please, can we go somewhere here or in your garden and talk for a while? There's so much I truly need to tell you about me."

She hesitated momentarily and thought, I'm not meeting with customers today. Bill is seeing to the guests who are leaving.

"The garden sounds perfect. Buster finished a couple of simple benches on the south side of the main house." She left the bundle in the car and offered him her hand. "This way."

The path was narrow and the bench not far from her large office window with its grand view of the sea. Frowning, she faced him squarely as they seated themselves.

"I couldn't imagine anyone would be watching me through that window." Her sharp tone caused Ernie to blush.

"It was thoughtless of me, and I apologize. There were so many wonderful places and things to explore whenever I was out here. It was quite by chance, and not a habit."

Feeling more at ease, they both turned their gaze to the calm water.

"Let me start with what's uppermost on my mind

related to these wonderful grounds. For a good while I've wanted to ask if I could rent your summer kitchen once a month for veteran meetings. We could be rowdy and free to sing or shout without bothering a soul. We bring food and occasionally cook hamburgers or frankfurters and always have coffee going. No need to give me an answer right now, but I wanted to get that off my mind. What's important related to me being with them is my being away from the Hollow for a couple of years in training school." Taking a deep breath, he waited for any reaction from Marie. She was silent. "You might understand, we veterans have a brotherhood, safely sharing what is difficult for all of us. A lot like the wonderful friendship you church ladies have."

"Communities of like-minded people are precious. I certainly know what you mean and will be happy for you to meet here. Cleanup and non-smoking would be required. No fee for you veterans. Our whole nation owes you fellows. You gone away for years? When is this going to happen?"

"Well, those plans are being pieced together." He looked away and changed the subject back to the veterans.

"I had our fellows on my mind when that wild situation happened at the open house. When the gunshot happened and fire was discovered, my guys might have frozen. I froze. I was embarrassed, watching Mrs. Winter run to the fire. I cringed at the thought of our group being unable to jump into action. It left me feeling sad and hesitant to ask about meeting here."

Marie allowed a comfortable silence before she spoke.

"I'm still curious about your plans to be away for

years. If you are not ready to talk about it, that's ok."

"Oh, no, I can fill you in with what I know for sure. To start at the beginning." He paused. "My experience in the Army as a medic was so satisfying and challenging, the thought of caring for the sick and wounded in civilian life never left me. Being a doctor wasn't realistic, but nursing as a career appealed to me. I recently applied to a long-standing program not far from here and got accepted. The wonderful part is how many other men have applied recently. I met two guys with Army experience like mine. The Director of Nursing who interviewed me let me know their school has always had men in the nursing school and that convinced me to sign up for the September class."

He spoke slowly, a faraway look in his eyes. Marie felt compelled not to interrupt. When he looked up, he saw a broad smile on Marie's face that warmed his whole being. The incoming tide tumbled a pleasing melody. The crackling sound of tires on the bed of old shells alerted them of someone's arrival. They walked to the front of the house and saw Howard and Annie with rose bushes and a shovel, quietly debating what spot would be best for the thorny flowers.

"Well, hello, Marie and Ernie. So good to see you two. Help us decide if we should leave the planting to Buster when he's here or do what I already told Howard, leave them with you. Ernie, are you helping out here today, too? Your helping hand at church was appreciated. Got us all out early and here we are, enjoying the rest of this lovely day."

Marie and Ernest left her question unanswered as Marie took the rose bushes, thanking her profusely.

"I know a good spot for them and will have Buster

put them in. He's still keeping Granny Araujo updated and runs ideas by her. Do you need to get home soon, or will you consider joining us for cool drinks? I'm not allowing any of you to do a bit of work out here today."

"We sure would love to join you Marie... and you, Ernie?" Annie answered. "Such a splendid idea."

Ernie agreed. "You can count me in, Marie. I'm not expected at my parents at any particular time."

The ice box was always stocked with cool lemonade or punch for guests, which allowed Marie to have everyone seated and served in minutes. Annie led the conversation with questions for her about upcoming projects while Howie quizzed her about the average number of guests and where they came from. Ernie sat quietly, beaming and listening.

"Well, many thanks, Marie for the hospitality. We should be heading home. Ernie, can we give you a lift or do you two have other plans?"

"No plans, Annie. It would be nice to hop in with you and Howie. Save Marie an extra trip into town."

Everyone rose to leave. Ernest calmly gave Marie a hug and assured her he would see her soon. Everyone was smiling as they went out the door.

Chapter Fifteen

At his request, Howard and Annie dropped Ernest at his sister's house. Claire was already opening the door at the sight of the car.

"Thank you for the ride," Ernie said as he hopped out.

"Hello, you two," called Claire. "How are you? Ernest, I thought you went to the B&B today."

The Sullivans waved a hello, goodbye as they continued on their way.

"That's where we came from, Claire. The Sullivans stopped by there, too."

Once they were inside, Claire continued a stream of questions.

"Have a seat, Ernie, and stay a while. Claire will simmer down. Stay for supper. We're about ready to eat."

Claire rolled her eyes heavenward but respected Mark's wisdom in welcoming instead of interrogating her brother.

"Claire, I was at Marie's. I'm so glad that folks like the Sullivans are still visiting and lending a hand at the B&B. They came to plant rose bushes. Marie is certainly independent, but it's hard for me to forget the end of the open house. I hope to be a regular visitor, too."

From the nearby kitchen, Ruth caught sight of Ernest. She stopped setting the table and shouted happily,

"Hi, Ernie. Tonight, we eat supper in the dining room. You're staying, aren't you?" Not waiting for an answer, she added another plate.

Claire released a loud sigh and asked, "How long do I have to wait before I hear how things went at the B&B?"

"Not that much to report, Claire. There was more happening at church than our quiet visit at the house. You'll be glad to know I did tell her about going to nursing school. And the veteran's group can meet in the summer kitchen. She won't let us pay a rental fee: courtesy for our service to the country. You folks have been generous offering to host us here."

Ruth carried a big bowl past them.

"Spaghetti!" He was the first to rise, drawing attention away from his visit.

"Your Dad sent over a couple of loaves of bread today. Ernie, he does that at least once a month. It's as tasty as the crusty bread from The Baker's Dozen. He says his secret is having a pan of water in the oven while it bakes." Mark gave Ernie a wink and followed him into the next room. Appreciation and consumption of food took over the conversation. When the cleanup began, Ernest pitched in with the women and Mark cleared away the table and put away the washed and dried dishes.

"OK, Mr. Bearse, hero of the day. It was a joy to see you and Marie teaming up at church this morning." Claire and Ruth regaled in the retelling of the church clean up. Ernest spotted Mark setting cards and a board game out on the big table.

"Oh, no cards or games for me tonight, Mark. It's time I headed for home."

"Ok, maybe next week? Well, the least I can do is give you a ride home. It's gotten cool and already dark. We can meet up like this any evening you're available, Ernie. It's always great when we can get you to stay a while."

***

Marie was meeting with Jenny when she mentioned the way Ernest spontaneously joined the clean up after the meal at church.

"He still attends regularly, but no early exit from the service into the hall." Jenny was pleased and amused by Marie's joyful recapping.

"I miss having folks at my house, Marie. It was so enjoyable when we met after the dealings with the bank. Do you think Ernest would consider having lunch with the three of us? I am all work these days. You're making me long for an informal get-together. Oh; oh, that wrinkle in your nose and squinty eyes... I've stumbled on something. You're questioning the wisdom? OK, Marie, tell me what I have ruffled here."

"Oh, Jenny, it's the idea of Bill and Ernie. They are both, well both...special to me. I am enjoying the adventure of getting to know Mr. Ernest Bearse. We've become buddies recently.

Perhaps a going away luncheon in September. He will be leaving the Hollow for three years."

"I see I've got some catching up to do. Leaving? I was happy to hear and see you are having fun at last, get-

125

ting to know a respectful young fellow. I've noticed him at the strawberry festivals and how he manages to be where you are."

"Yes, Jenny. His sister, Claire, has been promoting and is pleased with our budding friendship, but he and I... well, he and I are in no rush just to make his sister happy. We are finding our own way to whatever relationship works for us."

Jenny's raised eyebrow made Marie laugh.

"OK, Jenny, what's behind *your* frown?"

"Hmmm, I know that by September, you will let me know what *you'd* like to see happen. This is definitely a new situation. And by the way, where is he going in September?"

"It's not common knowledge yet, so I know you can keep this information close until his plans are solid. But it's clear to me he's already made the decision to go to training school to be a professional nurse."

"Now that's a new one on me. I have no idea what that entails. If you have no strong objection, I would like to have all of you over long before September."

The length and strength of their relationship made it easy to drift right into the business at hand: real estate.

***

Jenny was pleased to find both Bill and Ernest eager to accept an invitation at her place in honor of Ernest's acceptance to school in Worcester. It was Marie who could not give Jenny assurance that she could commit to a specific day so soon.

"Jenny, I am worried about Granny and have been

going to her house as often as possible. Soon after the president died, she told my folks she feared she had had a mild heart attack. She was seen by the family doctor, and he assured them it was nothing but old age and the beginning of natural decline. I'm not feeling very social and want to keep an eye on her. I would like another opinion. That hasn't happened yet, so I am pretty anxious and determined to make sure she is cared for."

"I hope she is doing better. Do you suppose her fears derived from the sudden death of President Harding? Granny is very serious about politics. What can I do to help? Another doctor may also see her as an old woman of color fading away. You're not likely to find a colored doctor who would look at her as kin. Have you confided in Ernie? He might take special notice of her complaints and make some suggestions."

"No, Jenny, like I said, I am not feeling very social. I did ask the church group for a good referral. The group is almost as upset about the politics as Granny is. My parents worry me. They are so easily influenced by what 'the doctor said'. I can tell it's more than her age."

It was the ladies at church who continued to lament the loss of their popular president.

"This Coolidge is so stingy, increasing our taxes and not improving anything," Polly exclaimed. "Harding helped everybody, and I don't think it so scandalous that he helped his friends, too."

"Things in Europe have never rallied since the war ended. I think we are in for some challenging times. I've kept in touch with my family members who still struggle in Ireland. The spoils of war have left scars on the lowly. Colonialism has not been kind." Bridget was as somber as Polly.

Ernest made a special effort to catch Marie before she dashed from church.

"You heading for the Hollow, Marie? I know how worried you are about Granny. You've been staying with her? I'd like to tag along if it's OK. I've missed spending time with you."

He did not wait for her answer but simply followed her to her car. She waved him in. The silence between them was somber yet not uncomfortable, but what they encountered at Granny's sent them into high anxiety.

"She's not answering her door!"

A note requested that visitors come to her son's home. The quick drive left Marie panting as if she had run on foot.

"Poppa, where is Granny?"

"Now calm down, Marie, she is in the hospital, where the doctor says she will get proper care. She took a bad spell, was yelling, combative and we had to get help."

Ernest reached for Marie's hand and calmly asked, "What hospital, sir?"

"She's in the Pocasset County Hospital on County Road."

Marie's eyes blazed. Stone-faced, she shouted at her father," You took her to the County poorhouse?

Ernest took her arm and moved them to the door. "Thank you, sir. We will be going there right now."

He led Marie to the passenger side, moved quickly into the driver's seat and assured her, "I know where that is. I know you are worried about Granny, but that anger, what provoked such anger? Take some deep breaths. You look ready to explode."

With a fierce glare, she answered. "The poorhouse, Ernest! An asylum!"

"We're going there. It's a small facility for women. She must have shown serious confusion. Let's not go there angry. We want to be her allies and see how they intend to help her."

"They got a careless doctor. He never intended to find out what was troubling her. Yes, I am angry with my parents. They knew I was staying with her and finding a good medical doctor to really help her, not put her out of sight in a sanitarium. I wish I had stayed with her today. They waited for me to be out of her house, to go to church. I just know it!"

The drive was not long. Ernest begged Marie to sit in the car before entering. "We can manage this, Marie, all is not lost."

The hospital clerk welcomed them warmly and summoned someone to guide them to Mrs. Araujo's room. He was a young man with a shock of blond hair, slicked back. His brown doe eyes were kind, and his white trousers and stiff white shirt looked brand new.

"We are a small specialty hospital, able to give special attention to each of our two dozen patients: individual care, including your mother."

"Mrs. Araujo is my grandmother, and what is the name of the doctor caring for her?"

The attendant directed his answer to Ernest in reaction to Marie's angry, tearful question. "We have two full-time physicians, physical therapists, as well as competent practical nurses." His slow smile seemed genuine, and he turned to Marie, offering more information and assurance.

When Marie spotted Granny, she left them and went

to sit by Granny, holding her hand. She began to sing a lullaby Granny had so many times sung to her. Limp and with closed eyes, Granny eased out a crooked smile. Her breathing was relaxed and regular.

"We gave her a light sedative to reduce her agitation." The young attendant was still in the doorway with Ernest, who had introduced himself as a close family friend.

"And what is your name, sir? Are you one of the LPNs?" Ernest was impressed by the young man's professionalism.

"No, sir, you will notice the LPNs wear nursing caps identifying their training schools. I am a nursing attendant. We support the medical staff in many ways. Ma'am, your grandmother does need to rest. It was necessary to place safety rails on her bed on admission. She responded well to the sedative. Try not to rouse her completely. We avoid using restraints whenever possible."

"Restraints?! Don't you *ever* restrain my grandmother." She moved to the doorway and repeated her direction in quiet yet threatening words. "Not ever, do you understand? I will find a way to get her into a medical hospital where they will find a way to *treat* her. What do they think caused this event?"

"I cannot speak for our physicians, but I will find the doctor on call to speak with you." His voice trailed off as he swiftly left.

Ernest went straight to Marie and enveloped her in his arms. In a soft voice, he declared, "The sweet, crooked smile you coaxed from Granny makes me think she has had a serious brain bleed: a stroke."

When the house physician did arrive, he confirmed

Ernest's conclusion. That was the only visit they made to Pocasset; Granny passed away before dawn.

Ernest never mentioned to Marie his other hunch: that Granny had been suffering from severe high blood pressure, which might have been treated if discovered years before.

After the funeral, it took Jenny several quiet meetings with Marie to mention the upcoming Labor Day holiday. Ernest was due to leave the following Monday.

"I would like to extend an invitation to all of the Holmes family," she said. "Do you think that would be a nice gesture? It would still be a modest amount of folks, only seven. Claire and Ruth might want to bring a special dish. I'll keep it simple, roast chicken, roasted vegetables, good crusty bread and butter. A salad would round things off and a simple dessert like a decorated, dedicated cake from Baker's Dozen."

Marie sighed. "Are you thinking about on the holiday itself? That will be good. No one will be working, and Ernest will be leaving the following week. Sorry I have not been of more help with planning. I've been trying to be civil to my parents while they deal with Granny's house. It never had to go on the market. A family in the Hollow begged to buy it 'as is.' It will need quite a bit of work, and clearing Granny's belongings has been heartbreaking. My parents know how hurt I still am by their hasty, careless decisions."

"I understand, Marie, you need not think about the cooking and such. I have been planning and biding my time to make it happen."

"I did enjoy a few days with Ernest and Virgie at the library. Ernie has been trying to educate himself, studying Latin. The nursing school let him know it was important that he know some Latin. He didn't take any languages in high school. I took Latin and French. I must say, the French has been useful. My Canadian guests appreciate my attempts to use my school version. August brings so many of them to the Cape. I think they close all the shops for the whole month, and they tend to make reservations a year ahead."

Jenny was relieved to be chatting with Marie. The women in the church group noticed her lightened mood when she shared Jenny' s thoughtful plans to have a small send-off dinner for Claire's whole family. The women had been a bit somber, following the death of the president, and they were respecting Marie' s sadness at the loss of her grandmother.

Now it was Claire who needed cheering up. "Gosh, I sure am going to miss him. Marie, it was so special that you are giving the vets your place to meet. In July and August, both Mark and I helped out with transportation and little things. The group is flourishing. Mark agreed to be a regular. Ernest is so happy. The older fellows have taken the lead gracefully and have assured Ernie the group is in good hands."

Ernest was no longer a regular at church services. When the coffee hours ended, he found ways to meet with Marie at her place. They walked the beach for hours without needing conversation. On rainy days, they gathered books Virginia had picked out for them. With Marie coaching, he made progress learning a useful medical Latin vocabulary.

September arrived still feeling like summer. The holiday brought throngs of end-of-the-summer visitors into town. Marie and Bill, (who continued to increase his days working at the B&B before the harvesting season peaked), found themselves challenged to get to Jenny's at the designated time. They were the last to arrive.

"Here they are, at last!" cried Jenny. "Ernest's family insisted on bringing hot bread for our meal. Hope you two don't mind, we already 'broke bread' and enjoyed lemonade. Butter won't melt on your bread but do join us before the main meal is on the table."

Conversation exploded as explanations and greetings danced among them.

"Any fancy feast will start with bread or rolls." Bill did not hesitate to elbow his way to the table and cut himself a nice chunk of bread.

Jenny was calling attention to the summery weather, while Bill focused on the change in the political climate. "Here it is harvest time and this new chap has cut the aid government has been giving to farmers for years."

Mark noted, "He hasn't done much of anything that I've noticed. Just sitting back collecting the new taxes."

When the compliments began about the food, Mr. Bearse got to reveal his secret, learned from a close Italian friend. "Brick ovens and a pan of water make the best bread," he said. "My friend and his family have been on the Cape longer than my folks. They were brought over from Italy to start digging the canal. His recipe makes many loaves, and I know it by heart. Never tried to change a thing-except for the brick oven."

"We are the lucky benefactors. You've found a wonderful way to share the bounty."

Before the main course was finished, the political talk prompted Ernest to explain how much he admired and respected the former president.

"Folks don't even know he pardoned all the young men jailed for not going to war. We took better care of the German prisoners of war than our own men who refused to be soldiers. I refused to use a gun. Luckily, they needed medics."

"I've noticed changes at the bank," Bill said. "Has anyone else noticed how individuals were once the only ones playing with the ups and downs of the market? Now the banks have joined. I plan to speak with Mr. Weatherbee about our bank. I don't want them gambling with my funds."

It was a rhetorical question that came up again later when he spoke privately to Jenny and Marie.

Ruth jumped into the rambling conversation as the other adults. "My fiancé is still running rum," she said. "No other job offers as much money, and there are not that many full-time job openings, but there's plenty of money flowing around here. I am working during summer, to keep busy and enjoy being out of the house. Marie, have you considered hiring extra help this summer? I've met college students who spend each summer here."

"Not yet, Ruth, but if next summer brings the same number of guests or even more, I will certainly think about it. Are you interested, Ruth? I'd love to have you be our first summer staff person. What are they paying? A student I met was not even from this country. She was a Spanish speaker in a hotel on Main Street."

Jenny quietly set Bridget's fancy bakery cake before them.

"Now that's one beautiful piece of pastry." Mark's eyes were focused on the message written in frosting, "To Ernie with Love."

The reality of the coming goodbye mellowed the group as everyone turned to Ernest to offer good wishes, good luck and wonderment about the adventure he was embarking upon. Darkness had fallen as people rose to leave. Bill, who had come with Marie, elected to walk to his nearby lodgings, so Marie felt unabashed by the tears that slowly bathed her face as she drove home.

***

Ernest made the effort to be in touch with Marie before the end of the week.

"Marie, do you know the person who delivers your mail? He is going to become an important person, because he'll be leaving my letters. At least once a week I will be writing to you," he assured her with his usual adoring smile. "No requirement for you to do the same. I know there will be new things for me to experience and I want to share them with you."

He was at her place to gather and return books to the library.

"My train leaves on Sunday, the last of the low fares that entice vacationers. I want you to feel free to let people know how I feel about you, but I want you to hear it first. I love you, Marie Araujo." He paused so she could see his serious expression.

She said simply, "I know." And handed him a small, wrapped box.

"What's this?"

"Well, open it and see. Devon and I did some research, so please be honest and tell me if I'm being, well, a bit ridiculous."

135

He stood transfixed at the sight of two identical engraved silver rings.

"I think it will fit. I've held your hand so many times since we met. They are friendship rings. That's what the engraving says, 'friends forever.'"

"Well, have I died and gone to heaven? Do I deserve this creative beautiful woman, this ring? You are indeed the most amazing human being I have ever met." His eyes were wide, his face glowing, his body still for what Marie thought was an eternity. He sat down. Marie took the box from him and lifting his hand, tried the ring on his right ring finger, smiling as it fit perfectly. He hurried out of the chair, took the remaining ring from her and fumbled his way to her right hand.

"I'm shaking, sorry, I'll get it. Whew, perfect."

Quiet gazing closed the day. Ernie sat for a while in the car he had borrowed from Mark before raising a hand to Marie and driving off.

Chapter Sixteen

October brought back the after-church luncheons and women's gab sessions. Marie made no show of her newly acquired jewelry, nor explanation for her cheery mood and quiet humming while she worked. Devon, per usual, worked close to her and joined in the humming. Polly could not contain herself.

"OK you two, what's going on? I've been holding my tongue long enough. Business has been really good all year, and there's a lot to be pleased about, but winter's on its way. You two are making us all wonder what has happened or is about to happen. Claire, help us out here. Do you know what's going on? I'm sure it has something to do with your brother leaving town. You let us all know how lovely that sendoff was that the real estate gal hosted."

"I don't have any information to give. It's up to Marie to share if she wants to. Ernie is away and says things are going well at the training school. I can tell you he was so cheery and delightful leaving, it made me feel good, not even knowing what or why. Seeing him happy was enough for me."

"Well, this is the reason, Polly," said Marie. "He and I are friends forever. It was a breakthrough for me, fol-lowing a long spell of sadness to realize I can love again."

"Love?" Mary Helen nearly whispered it. "Marie, I am so happy for you. I've been quietly pleased to see the change that has come over you. Dear Father in heaven, no more funerals, please."

Something instinctive in Polly allowed her to drop the subject, sensing no more needed to be said. Marie was happy.

***

With regular invitations to share lunch, Jenny kept in contact with Bill and Marie. It was at these lunches that Marie comfortably shared details.

"My first letter came from Worcester. Ernie promised he'd keep in touch. We are in a committed friendship. I know neither of you will be confused, when I say, 'friendship.' We are free to have as many friendships as come our way, but we are owning up to how much we love each other: no limits, no promises, simple honesty."

Bill frowned. "Now that's quite an arrangement. How did you come up with that? I would never think it possible. On second thought, it was like that with George and me, but unspoken. I'd like to think you and I have a similar commitment, though clearly without the lovelight I can see in your eyes. Congratulations, dear girl. I wish both of you the best."

Jenny held her comment and contributed a smile in agreement. When she and Marie were alone, she would have many questions.

Bill turned serious and went on to talk about his visit with the owner of their bank. "I had him swear to me he was not using our deposits to dabble in the fast exchanges on the stock market. Folks have so much money they are playing risky games of buying low, selling high, guessing what the next fellow is doing. If I even suspect or can confirm Mr. Weatherbee is toying with our savings or investments, I'll alert you to take your money to another stable bank or sew it in your mattress! Seriously ladies, I am watching him closely."

Correspondence

My Dear Marie, this lovely autumn will soon be winter. I've been warned, these hills in Worcester turn treacherous with snow and ice. I will not be getting home to visit once the snow falls. Nursing school students do not have weekends or holidays off. Our professors meet with us during the week and our on-duty skill practice sessions consume every day. The hospital chapel is available to us, but Sunday is not a day off for us or our nursing supervisors and nursing arts instructors. The probation period will end in March. Then our schedule will be more flexible. Until then, we are assigned days off, looking forward to a week off. It's all teamwork, so my time off will depend on agreements with classmates and supervisors.

It's during study hours I wish you were here. It's a sweet agony, missing you. I pray you have not forgotten your forever friend. My heart aches to see you and hear you. I confess, I was not prepared to miss you so terribly. I will scrutinize and barter my schedule to get a day or two before November.

Love forever, your Ernest

Time skipped by for Marie. Her schedule, filled with hosting, showing properties, fishing and meeting with church women, barely left time for writing letters.

"I can't believe Thanksgiving will be here so soon," she said to the church ladies.

Devon asked, "Well, busy lady, what are your plans for the holiday?"

"I know I have no reservations that week and have not committed to showing any property. It gives me some time to think about getting up to Worcester, if Worcester is not able to come to Hyannis." Marie's smile invited Devon to make more inquiries.

"Oh, your forever friend is hoping, planning, to come home for Thanksgiving?

"His program consumes most all of his time. It's not at all like college, when I looked forward to all the holidays and spring break. In Boston, I could even get away weekdays to go to a ballgame or a show."

"Nursing programs attract nuns," said Devon. "They give care at reasonable or no cost. Ever since you told us Ernest was training to be a nurse, I've inquired and looked into what professional nurses' training is like."

"Devon, I shouldn't be surprised. I know you enjoy research. Please, tell me what you learned about Ernest's school."

"Oh my, I didn't inquire about one school. You know Vergie the librarian, she was able to get me books from Florence Nightingale to the present day. So many early schools were started by nuns, religious orders devoted to care of the sick. That history has carried over to today's training schools."

"Ah, once Virginia discovers you're interested in research, not love stories or mysteries, she will overload you with every source available."

Claire interrupted their laughter.

"OK, you two, what am I missing out on? I'm already envious, Marie. You hear from Ernie and know so much more than his family. I mean more than I do. I cherish the first postcard he sent: a beautiful park. The note explained how demanding his schedule is." Claire was smiling yet her eyes were sad.

"Oh, Claire, I only manage to send letters once a week nowadays, and if a week goes by before I hear from him, I know he is on a new assignment or taking tests."

"The family is hoping he will get time off to get home for Thanksgiving. It seems he's at the mercy of his supervisor." Clair's melancholy expression returned as the conversation ended.

Because Jenny met almost weekly with Marie, she had the opportunity to ask what kind of news Ernest was able to write about that would be impersonal enough to share.

"He is very pleased with the flat he is sharing with other male nurses," Marie told her. "The strict rules the women have to abide by in the dormitory are not necessary with the men. Many of the women are right out of high school, just teenagers. Several of his roommates are older than he is. It seems medics and other veterans are attracted to the field of nursing and become pharmacists and anesthetists. I guess men are expected to be mature and responsible, while the female students need supervision and some kind of protection or control."

She told Jenny laughable stories, too. "Ernie near fainted when he assisted for the first time with the delivery of a baby. It frightened him so he was unable to move."

Jenny often found her busy and serious. "Marie, do you feel lonely these days?"

"Not at all, and I'll bet you don't, either. I still do a bit of fishing. The church women are closer than ever during these changing times. What made you think I might be lonely?"

"Well, no regular visits to the Hollow. Still keeping your distance from your parents. I know that's not new, but it is noticeable. I guess there's still big brother Bill. Your budding close friendship with Ernest seemed to get 'nipped' in the bud. I wondered."

With a mischievous grin, Marie said, "I actually do have a new friend I meet regularly: his name is Gabriel, the mailman."

Jenny remained serious. "Your mother and I have never been friends, but she chased me down at the grocers, almost blocking my way. She appeared desperate for me to listen to her concern. I'm certain she was sure I would see you before she would. Well, she didn't ask me to share her concerns but was hoping I would. I resented her putting me in the position of bearer of bad news, but I can see by your expression, it was the right thing to do. It's about your father."

"Poppa? Is he sick? Please tell me what's bothering her."

"No, he is not ill, but a bit 'sick' at heart. The two of them are miserable, not only because of Granny's passing, but your dad is convinced you blame him for the hospitalization. He not only lost his mother, but because of the way you feel, he believes he has lost you, too. Your Mother is guilt-ridden."

"Guilt-ridden? About what?"

"She says she nagged at your father and insisted he put Granny in the care of the County. Whenever you were not at Granny's, he spent all of his time there. It got on her nerves, and she could see Granny was not improving, so she demanded he get her to care."

"Oh my, oh my, Momma was never close to her old-world mother-in-law. I am somewhat relieved. I know how insistent my mother can be and how Poppa indulges her. It makes sense."

"Does this mean you will stop by before Thanksgiving?"

"It's something for me to think seriously about."

Jenny left feeling relieved that she had done no harm. After this somber conversation, Marie climbed the chimney stairs out onto the so-called widow's walk, gazing at the amazing view, speaking aloud, addressing the Sea. "You are simply another one of nature's underestimated, taken-for-granted gifts. Like us women, recognized as a source of life, containing many riches, sustaining life and on occasion, powerful enough to take life away."

***

"Good morning, Missus. Yes, I have mail for you." Gabriel's smile matched Marie's as she rushed to greet him at the door.

"More mail, more new faces. Your G&M B&B is a busy place. Your man, Buster, showed me the box he is fixing to hold mail: long enough to hold a newspaper."

"You will be able to leave our mail whenever I am not here waiting for you."

"Oh, I've left it with Buster on occasion. That's when he showed me the letter box he's fixing to fasten onto this side entry door."

"Mr. Shattuck is very reliable and as you can see, very handy with tools."

Gabrielle noticed how Marie referred to Buster as Mr. Shattuck. He had not forgotten the old caretaker as he used to be. The mailman smiled to himself, thinking, "Well, well, that old man has certainly become transformed. I'll be addressing him properly from now on."

Marie opened the letter from Worcester before she reached her office.

My Dear Marie, good news, Because I have only had half days off since September, me and my classmates conspired with our favorite nursing supervisor to allow a few students three days off at Thanksgiving. Those who do not have that holiday off will get their three days off at Christmas. If you were still considering coming to Worcester, hold off. My classmate, Paul Liccadone lives in Bourne. He will drive me to Hyannis. If you are up to it, you can drive me back after. Saturday or Sunday. We can have one day to ourselves. You could even stay over, rest at a hotel before going home. Letters take days to get back and forth. I'm figuring out how to reach you by calling Jenny's office. She's the only one I know with a personal phone. I am confident you two will see each other. I'll get details to her about possibilities and timing. Hoping to HEAR your voice soon,

Ernest, your forever friend ... longing to be yours forever.

The smile on Marie's face was still there when she entered the church hall on Sunday.

"It's nice to see you at peace, Marie." Devon greeted her with an observation. "You still getting out fishing? You look like you've been out in the sun. With a good-sized team of trusted employees, it gives you more time for doing things you enjoy."

"Having Bill and the loyal, cleaned up Buster Shattuck, along with several university students I've hired over the summer, gives me time to keep working with Jenny Small. We don't need to go to Boston or New York very often. Folks come here to my office or Jenney's to do business."

"Your long-distance buddy coming home for Thanksgiving?" Polly was convinced Marie's noticeably bright disposition involved Ernest.

"Well, Polly, that is a possibility that he is working out with others. All Hollows Tide and all the activities of October are long over. I'm sure Thanksgiving plans will be decided soon."

"Remembering our lost loved ones can be a sad time for most of us." Devon's serious tone darkened the mood.

"Well, your turkey will cost more this year. The prices of all farm products have risen." Polly was adamant.

Bridget's loud explanation got everyone's attention. "Well, you know why don't you? That Coolidge, that do-nothing president, cut the allotment all farmers have gotten for years. It's not like one can predict a drought. A good profit harvest one year can be a loss the follow-ing year. His vision is narrow and certainly blind when it comes to farmers."

Voices chimed in.

"The president is very content to leave most things to just muddle along. I wonder whose pocket the Farm Loan Act went into. It kept prices stable for years."

"That adjustment allowed farms to buy those big machines and to rotate crops."

Marie noticed the information that had the ladies riled up had been frequently mentioned by Bill Millett.

When the cleanup finished, Marie was the first to leave, going directly to Jenny's home office. "My recent letter from Ernie says he is quite certain he will be home for Thanksgiving," she said. "I need to talk with him. Out in the Port, we all use the phone at the Post Office. In the Hollow, we use the one at the Rexall Drug Store. With all the luxuries the Wallace family had, they evidently had no desire to own a telephone. Oh, balderdash, Jenny, until folks at church mentioned his name, I had no idea how much I miss him." Tears fell as she looked away. "We are friends and buddies, but he has become so important to me."

"Well, Marie, I think I know what we will be working on today. When do you plan to see your parents? Has there been any conversation about the holiday?"

"My parents? Have not even thought about them. Ernest is going to try and reach me on your phone. The possibility sent me straight here in hopes he had already contacted you."

They both heard a ringing. "I don't expect any business calls on a Sunday afternoon," Jenny said. "That ringing must be the call you were hoping to receive. Should I pick up and verify, or will you pick up and surprise him?"

Marie already had the telephone in hand.

"It must be him, that big smile behind those tears." Jenny turned to leave the room.

"Ernest, it's really you!" She gasped. "This is wonderful, it's like being in the room with you. Your last letter got me so excited and hopeful, and, oh, Ernest, how are you?"

"Couldn't be better, simply hearing your voice."

Marie could picture his beaming smile as she babbled on. It was quite a few minutes later when Jenny heard shouting and opened the door.

"Making plans for after graduation?" Marie's voice grew even louder. "Two years away and you've already made a job application to Hyannis Hospital? You want to know if I'll take a major role in all of your plans? Well, Mr. Bearse, that sounds an awful lot like a proposal. Surely you do not expect me to give you an answer. Not like this! Long distance! No answer long distance. You have ruffled my feathers into a knot. I am angry. I am happy. I am confounded! Ernest, I love you."

Ernest heard a soft click. Unable to move, he remained in the booth until the soft hum of the phone alerted him to hang up.

What have I done? Too excited to think properly? Most of us veteran students have solid plans for our next steps after graduation. By March, we'll all know we are fully accepted and on our way to graduation in the next two years. I have some explaining to do.

His next letter arrived in Hyannis quickly.

I am angry with myself for rambling on excitedly, forgetting to share how and why my plans have jumped two years ahead of our personal communications.

Please know that I am not impulsive. I simply cannot envision a future without you in it. We can end all this, be more conventional until we meet at Thanksgiving. It can wait. My half-spoken question is now known. Your answer is not required while we are both a bit upset and confounded. Please forgive the awkwardness and be assured, my love for you will not change no matter what you need to say or do. I remain yours forever, Ernest

At the church, Claire wasted no time in bringing up Thanksgiving plans.

"Bridget, will you have a sale this year on day-old bread? There have been years when you gave it away here at church, saving us planning to set aside any to be ready for stuffing."

"Timely question, ladies. I am sorry, but fortunate too, there won't be many leftovers of any kind this year. Business hasn't slowed down at all. Some customers have ordered loaves already, just to have a head start on preparing dinner. There's nothing like homemade stuffing. Anybody still making cornmeal stuffing?"

"How about we share our favorite recipes and maybe try something new this year? My favorite is still cornmeal, Bridget." Mary Helen invited everyone to swap ideas if not recipes.

"Anybody still making oyster stuffing?" Devon wondered.

"No, good old giblet, with a smidgen of onion, lots of sage and poultry spices."

Marie was silent and sober, while the group became more and more animated. The holiday was coming too soon.

Marie arrived at Jenny's in a solemn mood.

"Well Miss Marie, have you been in touch with your family yet? I got a call from your dear friend. He will be ringing this phone any minute. He knew a letter might not arrive before Thursday.

"Oh, yes, Jenny, I visited and ended up sleeping there shortly after that call from Ernest." Before she could say more, the phone rang.

"Ernest? I do believe I'm the one who should apologize." With eyebrows raised, Jenny almost ran out of the room.

"Ernie, you are so confident and honest. I was just, well, flabbergasted. My feelings for you have blossomed and bloomed and I hardly knew how much I have missed you." Ernest kept silent. "I must confess, I was not prepared to miss you so terribly. It shocked me and I got angry, irrationally angry at myself and directed it at you. Ernest, I'm not even sure I should expect forgiveness. You have gotten yourself involved with a very emotional woman."

He could hear the smile in her voice, and they both began laughing. Jenny could barely believe her ears, but was convinced things were going well. Marie knocked on the door to let her know when the call ended.

"Is there anything I should know about this doggone holiday?" Jenny asked. "Claire has generously invited me to their house. She had no idea if you two would be there."

"I do not have an answer about where Ernest and I will be eating Thanksgiving dinner. I let him know I've spent time at my parents. We never referred to the holiday. As a family, we used to gather at Granny's, lugging portions of the meal while she prepared the turkey, mashed potatoes and her favorite: turnip."

"What happened at your folks' house?"

"You might say we have turned a corner. All we did was weep together. Mother kept apologizing and Poppa cried tears like I have never seen before. He could only say he had done something he was afraid I could never forgive. When I could talk, I spoke with them separately. With my mother, when she ruffled through her dresser looking for a nightgown for me. Yes, I stayed overnight. All I had to say was I clearly understand why she got medical help for Granny. She hugged me so tight; I gasped for breath. With Poppa, all I had to do was look him in the eye and say that I know he had no choice and there was no need to forgive someone who did their very best and thanked him over and over for being at Granny's any day I was not there. His hug near broke my ribs! And he looked ten years younger when he stopped crying. I was so exhausted; I slept like a baby in my old room."

Before Jenny could say a word, the phone rang again.

"I'll grab that, I know it will be Ernest. There's no time for letters to help us figure out what we are doing Thursday."

"Yes, it's me. Thank heavens for Jenny. Will you be going to your folks for dinner? I've been hoping you would join my family, but if your parents are expecting you, mine will understand. It might be best if we go to your folks. The only time I've spent with them was that sad day we went looking for Granny. This will be an opportunity for us to get to really know each other."

Jenny remained transfixed, shamelessly eavesdropping.

"Perhaps Jenny and I can go by the house today and make a plan," said Marie. "Have your friend, Paul, leave you at my house. Things will be in place this week."

Jenny was beaming as she tiptoed out to the other room.

It was a very short conversation. Marie shouted, "I'm driving, Jenny. Let's get this over with."

At the Araujo house, the conversation wandered.

"Marie, we had not planned to do anything this Thursday," said her mother. "You well know, this was Granny's big day. It's just too soon. Too soon to be thinking of celebrating."

The look Mr. Araujo gave his wife was lethal. He grunted. "Life goes on, my dear," he said. "Let's make a new plan, a new tradition, right now! Here sits our daughter, we barely see her on any regular basis. She's here with a long-time family friend. Why, we've known Jenny since she was a child. We should be including her in our new tradition. I'm no cook, but we should be able to pull this off easily. All we need to do is roast a turkey and mash some potatoes."

"And those bitter turnips that need sugar just to swallow." Marie's mother sounded bitter herself as she pouted.

"Look, Momma, Jenny and I can do some cooking and carry it here, like we used to do to Granny's. I'll stay here in the Hollow. And please know my best friend, Ernest, will be coming." Her voice was almost childish as she pleaded with her mother. The dynamic was clear. Jenny shifted uncomfortably in her chair.

"Mr. Araujo, you can expect company this week, and all you need to do is set the table for four. I already have a dinner invitation, so I will have a chance to get in the holiday mood by cooking with your daughter." Her cheery voice made Mr. Araujo smile. With a gracious bow and wave at Marie, Jenny rose and headed for the door.

"Well, thank you, Miss Strong, for your generous offer. This is a difficult time for the two of us. Having guests might be a good thing." He gave Jenny a wink as the two young women left.

"Good heavens, Marie. Did the two of them bicker like that while you were growing up? I can see why learning to be an expert fisherwoman was so attractive."

"Jenny, I am so indebted to you for your generosity... and quick thinking! You got things wound up so elegantly, I hardly knew what happened. We better go shopping together tomorrow. You've given me a challenge. I've got a wonderful big oven, so I'm doing the turkey."

"OK if I contact Claire?" Jenny asked as Marie drove her home. "I can reach her on the hardware store phone. She will be glad to hear the news, Ernest having dinner with you and your parents."

"Jenny, you are one gem of a friend. Of course, give her the news."

Sometimes the best laid plans really do work out.

Jenny called to thank her hosts for their thoughtful invitation and inform Claire of Ernest's holiday plan: adding an unexpected remark. "This is a special honor for me to be your guest. Don't be surprised if your brother will be having a heart-to-heart talk with his future father-in-law. I can hardly wait to hear about Ernie's dinner."

Claire repeated the statement aloud as she hung up

and was scowling. Her daughter who happened to be in the hardware store, jumped for joy. It was closing time. Ruth had come along with Mark who was outside waiting to bring them both home,

"Mother, you are still frowning. Don't you get it? Maybe in the near future, we will be invited to a white wedding. My beloved uncle Ernie in his crisp white professional uniform and your sister-in-law in a beautiful white gown."

About the Author

Dr. Shirley F. B. Carter was born in Boston, Massachusetts during the Great Depression. She grew up in Worcester, attended College and University in Massachusetts and is a third generation Black Yankee. After marriage and raising children, she is now retired, residing in Worcester, near her extended family.